Ghost Portrait

Gregory Norminton

Ghost Portrait

SCEPTRE

First published in Great Britain in 2005 by Hodder and Stoughton
A division of Hodder Headline

The right of Gregory Norminton to be identified as the
Author of the Work has been asserted by him in accordance
with the Copyright, Designs and Patents Act 1988

A Sceptre Book

1 3 5 7 9 10 8 6 4 2

A CIP catalogue record for this title
is available from the British Library

Hardback ISBN 0 340 83465 X

Typeset in Sabon by Hewer Text Ltd, Edinburgh
Printed and bound by Clays Ltd, St Ives plc

Hodder Headline's policy is to use papers that are natural, renewable
and recyclable products and made from wood grown in sustainable
forests. The logging and manufacturing processes are expected to
conform to the environmental regulations of the country of origin

Hodder and Stoughton Ltd
A division of Hodder Headline
338 Euston Road
London NW1 3BH

Methought I saw my late espoused saint
Brought to me like Alcestis from the grave . . .
John Milton, Sonnet XIX

1680

She cannot read his face in sleep. Leaning closer, she tastes the sourness of his breath and wonders what colours blaze beneath those lids. His body holds no mystery for her; she is familiar, from shouldering its helpless weight, with the animal his soul is fastened to. But his eyes, when they open, are frosted like windows in winter. She smiles and they are surfaces from which her smile rebounds; a chamber to which she cannot find the key.

'Father?'

She has broken his sleep like a spider's web; he sighs to catch the shrinking edges. 'Oh – Cynthia.' Dried spittle gums his lips. He breaks the seal with his tongue and makes an effort to sit forward. He will not be considered an old man full of sleep.

'Have I woken you, Father?'

'I was resting my eyes. Your mother came to me. She rested in that chair and smiled. She was silent as ever, and the words she did not speak echoed in my mind like music.'

Cynthia has heard this lyric before. She notes the

dying fire. It needs more wood from the hall. He is waiting there. 'Mr Stroud is downstairs, Father.'

'What hour is it?'

'Past ten.'

'In the morning?'

'In the evening.'

'So soon? He has come so soon?'

'Immediately upon receiving your letter.'

The old man fills his lungs as one standing on a promontory takes in the sea air. He smiles, prelude to his only jest. 'Tell him I cannot see him. Tell him I shall see him now.'

He has shed his coat, which made him sweat as soon as he entered the house. The hall is warm and close, smelling familiarly of lavender and buttermilk and that mysterious perfume, like wood smoke and gorse flower, whose origin he has never been able to discover. Pressing his hands together to still them, he sees on the table a plate of Dutch biscuits (which, he knows, Cynthia bakes for her father's reminiscences) and the pastry coffin of the evening's meat. He realises, from the ache in his belly, that he has eaten nothing since midday dinner.

Upstairs, a door clears its throat. She is coming. He stares into the empty hearth, at the blackened fire-brick, for a moment not to think of her, of the urgent letter, by her hand, which he has folded in his pocket. It is a year since last he came to the manor: a year since he passed beneath the sprawl of the oaks and swept up their boughs with the wind from his horse. Is it the speed, the haste of his ride which shortens his breath? He hears her footsteps outside and the whisper of her dress as it sweeps the floor. He would look up at her entrance (already the door is creeping open) but he dares not alter his outward pose, meaning to seem ignorant, until she speaks, of her return.

'Mr Stroud – he will see you now.'

A turn of phrase, he thinks: force of habit. Acknowledging his hostess with a sideways glance, William rises and wipes his gloved hands on his hips. 'Thank you,' he says, and on the momentum of his standing finds the courage to meet her eyes. He receives no word from them. Cupping a hand about her taper, she leads him the familiar way.

Ascending the stairs beneath the bell of her dress, William is surprised by a desire to plunge his hands into it, as one bathes one's face in the petals of a rose, for the cool kiss of its living fabric. He sees, with a pang of redundant tenderness, Cynthia's pale hand as it grips and then skips along the gleaming banister.

'It is a strange hour,' he says, 'for you to play hostess.'

'We have become nocturnal creatures.'

'Then what of rest?'

'My father sleeps fitfully. As do I.'

William regrets the scolding tone of her voice; he tries to honey his own with a smile. 'As you must. When we are infants we shape our parents' world to our demands. When we are grown, the opposite is true.'

'He is my father. I owe him everything.'

'It is merely an observation . . .' Tenderness changes to anger in him; the anger is not at Cynthia. It finds a dark, introspective chord. 'And yet, you will allow, we do not *ask* to be born.'

'Nor do we ask to grow old.' Cynthia claims the vantage of the uppermost step. 'Do you rail at the fact of your birth, Mr Stroud?'

'Only at the conditions of it. Forgive me, madam.'

'There is nothing to forgive.'

Candles burning on a pewter dish absorb the glow from Cynthia's taper. William knows the voices in the wood; he has waited many hours, on this dark landing, to hear the imperious summons. Now Cynthia listens at the door. There is a tendon straining in her neck. He watches the shadows dance on her face and notices how, for all her refinement, she continues to breathe, like a child, through her mouth. He reaches impulsively for her hand on the latch, then stubs out his fingers against the door.

'You are very formal with me, Cynthia.'

She looks at him but says nothing; then she knocks and together they enter her father's study.

'Mr Stroud, Father.'

William bows thoughtlessly. He has ridden two miles from the mill in a sort of stupor; then, at the front door, the presence of his hostess distracted him from the coming encounter. Surely, at this instant, he is dreaming at his desk and this active self is his spirit's emanation? 'Good evening, Mr Deller.' And for want of something else to say, he asks foolishly, 'I hope you are in health.'

'At my age one is lucky to be breathing. Health is an added luxury.'

The voice sounds the same, with only a faint obstruction to weaken it; but a haze has settled across the old man's face, a terrible vagueness spreading, it would seem, from his useless eyes. William smirks to acknowledge the quip, then remembers himself and, through his nostrils, forces a sough of merriment. 'Then I hope I find you in luxury.'

The vacant orbs turn abruptly from his voice. William finds alarming the speed with which they locate Cynthia. 'Daughter – are there cakes ready?'

'Yes, Father.'

'Go to the kitchen. Fetch us sack.'

'Very good, Father. Mr Stroud.'

William remembers to reverence as Cynthia withdraws. He watches the door close after her. She was to have been his intercessory. Now William looks, in the dim light from a dying fire, at the ancient face raised in expectation of his company. Unwillingly he is reminded of the tortoise he saw once in Dover. A midshipman prodded it with his pipe-stem where it stood, sluggish on papery claws, on a tavern table, and William saw the ancient stubborn face, the beak a patrician overbite glued at the jaws with saliva, and the eyes so dry, so wearily conditioned to obstacle and disaster, that he wished it had not been smuggled to England.

'Will you not sit, Mr Stroud?'

William frowns to chase the memory. Long ago – four years, is it? – when Mr Deller first spoke of his affliction, he worried that, in his optic blindness, the old man would more readily be able to see into his mind. Knowing the idea to be fanciful, he struggled all the same to keep himself free of base or disrespectful thoughts.

'Is it very dark in the room?'

'It is a dark night, Mr Deller. The moon is hidden behind clouds and is dwindled to a sliver.'

'I have little notion of time these days.' There follows a silence with no cracking of embers to occupy it. 'How is your work?'

'Well enough, sir.' Mr Deller gasps and appears to settle back in his chair. Is that a smile? William wonders. Is there mockery in his features? 'Do you mean the work I must or the work I *would* do?'

'I should allow no such distinction.'

'You know it exists.'

'Any commissions?'

'Lately I painted Squire Tate's prize sow. He would not have me paint Mistress Tate – though she railed at him from every window – since she is expected to endure somewhat longer than the pig.'

'Ah.' Mr Deller laughs: it is almost a breath. 'Men have painted baser subjects, Mr Stroud, and been ennobled for their efforts.'

'On the strength of mine it seems I am to paint a new sign for a tavern.' What is this anger in him? He has been summoned to the chamber of a dying man – a man who once eclipsed William's own father in his affections – yet he cannot shift this rancour from his breast.

'Mr Stroud, as you remember, when I had the use of my eyes, I saw much promise in your work.'

'And I was most glad of it.'

'You've a fine eye for natural form, an easy commerce between eye and hand, a good mind to work upon all.'

Their first meeting: William but a stripling, who relieved his chores with a stub of charcoal and some pilfered baking paper, and the celebrated painter, newly settled in the parish, more splendid in his doublet of cloth of silver, in billowing sleeves and breeches of black velvet, than ever William's father on a Sunday; a potent emissary from the world of power, transposing as by magic the mill, the mill-stream with a horse drinking and the green battlements of oak beyond, to a narrow square of canvas. William remembers the tent of white linen stretched between hawthorns above the painter's head; a peasant boy holding a quiver of brushes; the pricking of his scalp as the pale bewigged gentleman, murmuring kind encouragement, inspected his timidly offered drawings.

'My daughter used to anticipate your visits with great pleasure. Did you know that?'

William says nothing. As of old, he feels exposed without the language of gestures.

'You have maintained an acquaintance with her?'

'In all honour, sir.'

Mr Deller seems to grow, to inflate with sudden energy. 'Mr Stroud,' he says, and William, like a schoolboy caught dreaming by his master, straightens in his chair. 'The country is no place for a young artist. There is no challenge – neither rivalry nor comradeship. I fear your talent may be going to waste here in Kent.'

William stares at the ravaged face, at the lines of mirth and grief about the sightless eyes. 'What do you mean, sir?'

'Why, that tavern signs are useful things and good salary for journeymen. But you are no journeyman. I would not have tutored you else.'

William feels his heart constrict. Has the old man a position for him? An opening with a patron? 'There is my father's mill,' he says, 'which as you know I am bound to inherit. So the duties of a son keep me from my favoured profession.'

Mr Deller seems not to hear. 'When I have spoken, I would ask you not to be too hasty in your response.' Again silence, while a mechanism obeys its imperative, the cogs of a long-held resolution turning. 'I have, among my possessions, an unfinished portrait. Of my late beloved wife. I have called you here . . . in the hope that you will complete the painting for me.'

Disappointment masters William's breast. It is supplanted by trepidation. 'This portrait, sir. Is it the background you would have me finish?'

'It is the foreground. It is the subject.'

Mr Deller's wife? William cannot recall her name. Never, in all his years of tutoring, did the old man speak of her. 'You do me great honour, Mr Deller. But I fear what you ask of me is not possible.'

'What do you know of possibility?'

'Sir, I know that a portrait, if it is to be a faithful likeness, cannot be made without the sitter. Or at least, a representation of the same.'

'The representation is exact and perfect in my mind.'

'And how would I go there to fetch it? With all the will in the world, both yours to give and mine to receive, I cannot be privy to your memories.'

'The canvas is not blank. The ghost of an outline, at least . . .'

'I cannot.' William clenches his jaw until his mouth fills with bitter water. He regards his calloused hands in the embering light. 'Mr Deller – sir – I would not be able to give the mark of *life* to those lines.'

'She has been dead for twenty years. The woman I studied and cherished, whose every line and blemish was my landscape . . .' The painter is agitated, leaning forward on his chair. Does he *see* through those frosted spheres? Only active eyes, surely, could so penetrate a man? 'Do not tell me, Mr Stroud, that this portrait cannot be completed. It *must* be.'

'In which case . . .'

'Sir?'

'You must seek out other eyes and hands than mine. I am sorry.'

'Then give me your help!'

'I may not.'

'There shall be fit reward, Mr Stroud.'

A gust of wind snores in the chimney. Both men sit listening to the night, to the sound of each other breathing like wrestlers after a struggle. William needs to hear it said. Though the old man cannot see him, he adopts a look of innocence. 'I would that I followed you, sir.'

'I have little time remaining. I must make provision for a future other than my own . . .' Mr Deller leans against the back of his chair: it is the studied opposite of a conspiratorial crouch. 'If you assist me in restoring the mother, you shall earn all rights to the daughter.'

1660

He is in the shallows of sleep when a dream disturbs him. His father is standing above him in the hayloft, a small cloud, a wisp of turbulence, cupped in his hands. He cannot see, in his dream, what the cloud consists of but clearly his father is weeping. With a cry the boy wakes, bitterly grieving his mother, three years dead, whose face he is beginning to forget. Poor Jem, he tells himself, caressing his brow. Sleep, Jem, hush-a-bye. And he turns his back to the stable door, whence a faint breeze tugs at his shirt: the breath of a storm brewing, which means to keep him in cold, unmothered wakefulness. No: he is mistaken; the rain has begun already to fall. He hears it on the roof, like a cloth being dragged across a floor, while beyond the trees and grasses softly whisper.

There is no time to make these sounds comforting. A noise detaches itself from the rain, of horses running. Of one horse, rather, coming from the road. Jem fumbles for the lantern. He fails to light it with his brother's flint and runs out to the yard. The sky is turbulent as in a dream; and indeed he is not yet fully awake as the foaming horse careers into view from behind the hawthorn. Where does this strange light come from? Is it the moon glowing through the clouds?

The rider sees Jem – the stables – the master's house. He pulls violently, too violently from the horse's shudder, on the reins and slows. Jem has heard his father greeting strangers. He shapes his voice in his throat before he calls. 'What news on the road?'

The rider is darkly cloaked, his hat pressed tightly on his head. 'Nothing good. I've not dismounted since Dover.'

The horse's eyes bulge in the storm light; thick cream drips from its mouth. Jem reaches tentatively for the bridle. The steaming presence of the horse and the unknown, brooding man upon it are stark intrusions on his fancy. The world has come to him, smelling of action. Young though he may be – a fool, his brother says – yet he knows what today is. 'Has the King landed?'

The stranger dismounts on Jem's side and stands, bow legged, pushing his fists into the small of his back. 'I saw him myself. There were crowds to greet him. They lifted their arms and cheered. I thought I'd be sick from the smell. Such a frenzy for a peruke suggests we *deserve* to be ruled by one.'

Jem looks, uncomprehending, at the bitter cast of

the stranger's mouth. He would have liked to have been there, in the festive streets. He imagines the nearness of the sea; the fret of sailing masts above the rooftops; cries of gulls and cries of welcome. 'What is your name, sir?'

'Thomas Digby.' The man's face, shadowed by his rainswept hat, seems to arrange itself to an uneasy softness. Jem hears kindness, wilfully inflected, in his voice. 'And you, friend?'

'James, sir.'

'Be as familiar with me as with yourself, James. I'll brook no deference, do you hear?'

'Yes, sir.'

'Not *sir*.'

Jem thinks he has angered him. The rain grows heavy; it drums on the boy's skull, making him feel more stupid than he knows himself to be. He pulls the wet bridle and gingerly strokes the horse's cheek. He wants to soothe it after its too-hurried race. Keeping his eyes on the animal – which will follow him meekly to the stable – he finds the courage to question its rider. 'Was he handsome, sir? I should like to set my eyes on a king. See what all the fuss is about.'

Damnable rain: Digby must shout to be heard above it. 'Believe me, the sight is not worth the expense of its maintenance. Cherish instead the smiles of your children.'

'I'm only a boy, sir.'

'Then cherish your freedom while it lasts.'

Jem points, needlessly, the way to the house. It is grander than Thomas Digby imagined: the ground floor of Maidstone flint, the upper walls handsomely beamed with gabled windows, and five chimneys feebly smoking against the deluge.

'He *is* in, I take it?'

'I saw him in the garden this afternoon, sir.'

Digby gropes in his coat pocket for a coin and presses it into the boy's hand. He watches as his horse is led to its rest. He sounds the depth of his hunger, his trepidation, and strides resolutely towards the door.

The path sucks at his boots as he enters the gaze of the house. There are trees, obscurely gathered, buffeted by the storm. Digby glimpses the brick of a walled garden behind dark topiary. There is a lake – is it? – to the side of the house; hence the music of rain on water. He pauses with his hand on the door knocker. There is no question of escape now, of seizing his exhausted horse and riding back at once to Lambeth. The pelting of the storm dictates his action; and from this Digby takes courage, for Providence seems to mean him to stay.

His knocking sounds feeble: a damp exclamation against the deaf and impassive house. A grille opens and a man asks him his business. Digby answers briefly, squinting to see who the man might be. Of course, *he* would not answer the door himself.

'We expect no visitors,' says the servant.

'I have made no appointment,' shouts Digby, 'but come on urgent business. He will be glad to see me.' Candlelight obscures the servant's face. Digby despairs of the black aperture. 'Let me *in*, man, I am soaked to the bone.'

'Wait,' says the mouth, and the grille closes.

Digby longs to pound the door with his fist. He buries a fingernail into his palm until his mouth waters at the pain. At length there are two voices within. He recognises the deeper voice and wonders whether he ought to take a step back, not to seem presumptuous when the door opens.

Two latches are lifted – a bolt slides aside. There is a shaft of light, of candles expiring, and a thickset figure fills the doorway. Thomas Digby removes his hat.

'*Bless me.*'

'Nathaniel.' He looks at the householder. The years have been good to him. A country squire, he is fat, almost jowly, with the ruddiness of good meat in his cheeks. How pale a figure must Digby make by comparison, bedraggled like a tomcat in the rain? Digby tries to smile, and something resembling a reverence possesses his limbs. When he looks up, the shadowed face has absorbed some of its surprise.

'Well – good God – what brings you here?'

'I was in Dover when I heard men speak your

name. They said you'd inherited the manor in this parish. Gentrified yourself.'

Rainwater falls in pulses from the eaves: spasmodic bursts, as if from the manor's arteries. Digby looks, under wet-beaded eyelids, at his portly host, whose amazement will keep him out in this storm. He knows that he is a spectre, the past's emanation, lacking as yet the substance, deserving hospitality, of one living. For remedy he feigns a sneeze and Nathaniel seems to remember his manners. 'Come in, Thomas,' he says, making a lordly sweep of his hand. 'These are foul times to be travelling.'

The despot's son – fledgling despot himself, with his French fripperies – back on English soil. Everything blasted, befouled; God's will confounded. 'Foul indeed,' says Digby.

'I mean, of course, the rain.'

Digby enters, averting his gaze from the ancient servant who kept him in the storm. He sees panels of burnished oak; the ruffled flames of candles; a great chest covered by a Persian rug. Tapestries resettle, expelling the wind he brought with him. There is a smell of wood burning, of thyme and sweet basil. This is a refuge, Digby thinks, where a man may believe the world to be good.

'Frederick, bring our guest a cup of hot wine. And tell Lizzie to prepare the table.'

The servant withdraws, dragging his withered legs.

His master looks distracted; with what may be nerves, he brushes his palms together. Digby glimpses the fine and tapering fingers, the cuticles stained a dirty yellow.

'You had a hard ride of it,' Nathaniel says.

'I thought I would outspeed the storm.'

'At your back, was it?'

Digby nods and, for want of words, pulls as it were a mask of water from his face.

'You must be cold, Thomas. Come through and dry yourself. We have a fire blazing in the hall.' Nathaniel clears his throat, without satisfaction, for he continues to rake at phlegm as he leads Digby down the corridor. Before the door a man rises to greet them. Digby recognises himself reflected in a large gilt-framed mirror. He notes with a kind of satisfaction the gloss of rain on his coat and the rider's glow of his cheeks. There is an angry welt on his forehead from the rim of his hat, too tightly forced.

'Uh – let me offer you a change of clothes.'

'No need,' says Digby. 'A good fire and your company shall warm me enough.'

In the hall a servant girl, dusty-aproned, with smallpox scars on her cheeks, rises and curtsies, leaving her bellows to sip from the hearth. Thomas Digby fights his dismay to acknowledge her; he fails to ignore her full rump as she returns to her stoking.

'The fire looks well,' says Nathaniel. 'Attend to our guest's supper, Lizzie.'

'Please,' says Digby, 'I am not in the least hungry.'

'You must be.'

Digby, lying, shakes his head.

'Are you certain you will eat nothing?'

'Thank you, Nathaniel, no.' He sees the open face of the girl as, hovering, she awaits instructions. 'A little bread, perhaps.'

'And cheese,' says Nathaniel, 'and the roast ham from the still room.' Digby's host coughs into his fist – successfully this time, for something is dislodged which he swallows with a grimace. Then, smiling feebly, he motions to a chair.

The hall is richly furnished, a haven of polished wood, with cherubim carved in walnut and a fireplace depicting sweet rural dancing, an easy harvest, swains at rest under spreading oaks. Digby does not sit down. He paces the room, humming to appreciate objects barely seen, achingly aware of Nathaniel's presence.

'Oh, Thomas, your restlessness wearies me. Please sit.'

'I was in Dover.'

'Yes?'

'To welcome Charles Stuart.'

Nathaniel says nothing and at length Digby must look at him. What is this tabard, the colour of sackcloth, that falls below his knees? How can he live in such a house and yet use a rope for a belt? Nathaniel catches Digby's frown and looks down at his front. His large fingers brush his chest as though sweeping crumbs. 'I had forgotten I was wearing it.'

'You had no overall – as I remember – on the common.'

'I finish work at sundown.'

'Is it to protect your handsome clothes?'

'Ah, the *kandeel*.'

Digby and his host silently watch the old servant, Frederick, fill two goblets with steaming wine. Digby's mouth waters in anticipation but he moves with deliberate slowness, a casual gratitude, to take his goblet. Frederick withdraws – so slowly, as if to his grave – and Digby scalds his lips on the spiced liquid. Feeling it descend, such a pleasurable burning, he breaks his silence.

'Surprised, are you?'

'Yes.' Nathaniel speaks too hastily. 'It has been a long time—'

'Ten years.'

'Ten?'

'Nine since your letters stopped.'

Digby watches his words strike home. Nathaniel straightens to absorb them; some discomfort makes him arch his back and wince.

'There will be reprisals, Nathaniel – you know that.'

'With the King restored?'

'A man cannot reach an accommodation with his father's murderers.'

'Well then, we have nothing to fear.'

Nathaniel rises, pushing back his plangent chair, and turns to the fireplace. He stands with indecisive, clenching and unclenching fists, his back rudely turned. When he bends to pick up the fire poker, Digby's bowels flutter. For an instant he thinks Nathaniel will strike him. But the heavy, opaque form crouches to disturb the burning logs – conjuring unnecessary sparks.

Keeping his back turned, Nathaniel asks, 'Do you still live in Deptford?'

'Lambeth.'

'Of course. Your old profession?'

'What service I can render my fellow men.'

'Good.' Nathaniel hangs the poker and turns, rubbing his hands on his apron. 'People need apothecaries. They are happier than your nobility who must die for the privilege of a surgeon's intervention.'

'Oh,' says Digby with a shiver, a dose of bile perhaps, racking his system, 'they die with me too.'

'But not by your hand.'

'By my leave. A good many.' Digby drinks, more

cautiously this time, the spiced wine. 'It's worse than in London. Men are crammed like rats surrounded by a mire . . .'

'I have lived in Lambeth.'

Digby gapes: 'I had forgotten.'

'They were lean times. Before we met. I could not afford my lodgings in St Martin's Lane.'

'Perhaps I saw you there?'

'You would not have known it was me.'

Digby sucks his teeth and looks at the ceiling. 'And now you live in this mansion.'

'I lost my brother and gained his inheritance. It is not by *my* labours that we live so well.'

Now Lizzie returns with cut bread and a sweating ham. Nathaniel's relief at the interruption is evident, however he may hide his face in shadow. Digby for his part salivates to see the meat – a luxury for those he tends to – its grey surface peeling to pink under Lizzie's knife. Like this spiced wine, it brings him pleasure and unease. There are consequences to plenty that no dentifrice in a bowl, or vial of juniper for the toothache, will remedy. But great hunger is upon him. He eats quickly, passionately, his appetite swelling with each bite, his lower teeth encountering upper crust, his tongue and incisors sinking into tender flesh. Slow down, he tells himself. Disguise your hunger.

'Why are you here, Thomas?'

Does he mean to ask this when his mouth is full? When he is disadvantaged? Digby chews slowly to think of his answer. 'To see you, Nathaniel.'

'But there must be a reason beyond that.'

'There are reasons . . .' Digby grips his food, elbows resting on the table. He looks in vain for some expression on that obscured face. 'I cannot see you, Nathaniel, with the firelight.'

'Forgive me.' To Digby's surprise, his host moves at once, relinquishing his advantage. A pang of sorrow makes Digby look down at his fingers: to see how the years have changed them. Had he passed Nathaniel in the street, would he have recognised him at all? He feels the scrutiny of those self-approving eyes. Some of their caution spreads, as a damp mist, to Digby's breast.

'Well,' says Nathaniel, 'you must eat and refresh yourself. Dry your clothes by the fire. Whatever we have to say, it can wait for such courtesy . . .'

1680

What inkling has he of a vocation? William would not pretend to possess a richer vision than his neighbour; yet he believes that matter is deeper and more intricate for him than it is for his taciturn father. Even today, in the mill, William may be stopped in his work by the grain of wood in a crossbar, discovering fragments of birds and beasts, nebulous chimerae. He sees the patina of corn dust left on the hopper when sunlight enters the stone floor, and doubts the world's impermanence. Is this infantile, a failure to cloud the eye with maturity? Yet he would not relinquish those moments when, like a gift, or a drift of shadow from a hillside, the richness of the meanest thing is revealed to him. When he was a boy he liked to walk with his eyes half shut. Faltering steps in the yard, in the high wind of a spring morning. Taking in the shift of forms, the fluidity between objects. The world transfigured by the veil of his eyelashes.

'Take those that please you, Mr Stroud. I have Cynthia read from the Bible. Nothing else can serve me now.'

William walks along the shelf, his candle dredging up from the darkness the faded spines of familiar books. He strokes the leather hide of Norgate's *Miniatura* and remembers smuggling it home in sackcloth to escape a questioning from his sisters. 'I could not take anything, sir.'

'I had rather they lived with you than died with me.'

As a young man, with a sense of promise burgeoning inside him, William used to climb to the bin floor at the very top of his father's mill. There, sitting on the ledge between the bins, feeling the great machinery stilled beneath him and the familiar mild sway of its anchored bones, he would open reverently (blowing flour from the pages) his tutor's books. The window latch was raised for light; the struts of the governors cast a shadow on his page; and there was the luminous pleasure of looking from the writing – that private world – to the pastures and woodland outside. Up here he could see his mother feeding ducks in the pond; white doves settling and scattering; his youngest sister Judith, who was to die at Christmas, waddling to break a huddle of sparrows.

'Thank you,' says William, 'I will borrow a couple.' He sets on their sides the Norgate and Peacham and remembers how, months into his training, with growing confidence from his lessons, he would sit, with a grain shovel on his lap to rest his paper on, trying to sketch the little rectangle of landscape, the family house and adjacent barns, the neighbours' field on the western flank of the hill. He would listen to labourers in the threshing barn as they winnowed the grain, and thought how like smoke was the chaff that escaped through the open doors. There was always variety in his subjects, depending where the post-mill had been turned to catch the wind. At rest, he thought, the mill was like a galleon in harbour, all rigging set loose. How intimately he knew its creaks and groans: intimations of a latent power that seemed to echo his own. To be set free from his duties to his father, to catch sail on the winds of chance and achieve some earthly purpose!

'Help me up, Mr Stroud.' William takes hold of Mr Deller's hand and grips his bony elbow. Nothing remains of his former brawn. It is like righting a bird. 'The chest, by the window.'

Leaning on William's arm, as though preparing for an imminent leap, the old man sets his jaw where he would go. It is troubling to support this dwindled figure, the skin of whose hands has shrunk to parchment, whose body smells of sack and urine.

'Do you recognise it?'

William looks at the large, walnut chest. He has not forgotten the breastplate inside, or the metal head of a halberd, its rusty edge mistaken for blood. Those were wonders for a boy accustomed to billhooks and winnowing baskets. He remembers the human skull, chop-fallen, and the stuffed birds on wooden perches, and a sherbet spoon from Istanbul with a string of pearls about its handle.

'I could find what I seek,' says Mr Deller. 'But the ground, you know, is very far down.'

Obligingly William falls to his knees and unlocks the chest. By the light of his candle he sees papers, a shale of documents, tattered portfolios and parchment. No trace remains of the old properties: their owner has no need of them.

'Do you see a red leather pouch with wooden bindings? Give it to me.'

There follows a clumsy shuffle to the hearth. Mr Deller demands to know the quality of the light. He seems exasperated, panting as he speaks. 'I only feel the heat and that barely, for I am grown as cold as a lizard.' Three ribbons bind up the leather pouch. The old man's fingers are soon embroiled in the knots and William tries to intercede. 'God's mercy! To be so helpless.'

'They are very tight. Permit me . . .'

But the old man will not yield. William holds the pouch for him until, after much fumbling and plucking at strands, the ribbons are loosened. At once, as though a catch has been released on a mechanism, Mr Deller steps back; he takes a deep, calming breath. 'What do you see?' he asks.

They are drawings: dozens of drawings, in pen and wash of bistre, in red and white chalk. Some are rough sketches, drafts for a painting; others, landscapes and interiors, are closer to finished works.

'Has anybody seen these, sir?'

'None but you.'

William feels like the robber of a reliquary. He handles with care the tinted papers. A few swift lines evoke a lake – its wind-ruffled reeds and sedge, a murky clump of alder. Here is the blacksmith's house in the village, here the village pond with white flurries of waterfowl. A young man, his face hidden by the brim of a most familiar hat, sits at an open window drawing, while the cursory smudge of a gardener's face passes outside. Again and again, William discovers studies of the manor: hushed and huddled interiors, the winding staircase of the kitchen easefully conveyed, a diaphanous figure warming itself by the stove. The house is filled with ghosts, it seems, faceless people bent over their tasks: afterthoughts to the architecture, whose beams and lintels are visible through their bodies.

'These are, uh, late works?'

'Late works,' echoes Mr Deller, his vacant eyes roving. William opens a folded paper to find drawings of Cynthia sleeping, of Cynthia absorbed in a book. He is stirred by tender and sorrowful desire. Cynthia stands at the kitchen table dicing vegetables, while old Lizzie works beside her, tousled and flour dusted, her curious eyes nudging at the artist's sketch-board. 'Do you see those women teaching a child to walk?'

'Oh, yes.'

'That is Belinda.'

William contemplates the drawing. The young woman's face is lightly sketched, with hatching for shadow on her turned cheek. Does Mr Deller expect him to use *this* as his model?

'It is the one drawing of the set that does not belong there.'

'Because it is older?'

'All the others were taken from life. But my wife never saw our daughter.' William feels a tightening of his skin. Mr Deller is inveigling him into his confidence. He will show William these last things to trap him in pity and obedience. 'It is a fantasy in which she still lives.'

William unpeels his gaze from the drawing to find Mr Deller groping his way along the wall. He pushes at a panel with his shoulder, using all his strength. The panel sighs and retreats to expose a secret compartment.

'An old priest hole,' Mr Deller pants. 'I made the discovery by chance . . . one day . . . stumbling to put on my breeches.'

William laughs with nervous amazement. What is

this sepulchral chamber? It is filled with soft tomb-stones: five paintings hidden under woollen shrouds.

'My last paintings,' says Mr Deller. 'You may take them. Perhaps, after my death, some nostalgic patron will give good money for them.'

'Oh, I could not sell them.'

'Anyway, they are yours.'

Feeling his way with uncertain steps, Mr Deller stoops into the alcove. William cannot resist the urge to offer him a guiding light; but the old man sees with his fingertips, stroking the corner of each canvas to count the pins stuck there as markers. William surmises from the dust that Cynthia is ignorant of this priest hole, or else she is forbidden to explore it. His light is the breath of wind that stirs a sealed tomb.

'It is the eye of the beholder, Mr Stroud, that gives life to a work of art. Unseen, it is unseeing. Now you may rescue these from blindness.'

Mr Deller sets a particular canvas to one side; the others he uncovers. William's eye is drawn to two paintings of Cynthia. In one she is Flora, dressed in a white and distinctly vestal gown, her hair garlanded with cornflowers and poppies. But this is no conventional portrait with classical trappings. Cynthia is coyly apprised of her dissembling. Incongruously she rests at the kitchen table, her left hand toying with a pair of garden shears. As with its neighbour (Cynthia ensconced, knees drawn up to her chest, in a seat beside the fire, her lips gently parted as she reads from a psalter), the goddess inhabits a hushed and candlelit interior. So too the bald labourer eating peas from a bowl, his expression null from chewing, his eyes touched with pure lead white to suggest a guarded and work-doused spirit. In all three paintings, objects are kept to a minimum; there is no superfluity of detail; the background is negligible, an earthy wash. The paint is roughly applied, so that, where clothes are coarse or hair unkempt, it almost tangibly conveys their texture, being kneaded and clotted or worked in with the fingers.

'And you will recognise this handsome fellow.'

Guided by the pins, Mr Deller unveils a small, murky portrait. William brings his candle up to it and his host stares back at him – the image of his host, rather, wearing a red turban and hempen work clothes.

'A far cry, would you agree, from your obsequious courtier?'

In his self-portrait, Deller's eyes have begun to cloud over. Is this why everything but the centre of his face is vague, a throbbing blur, like the air quaking about a naked flame? William thinks the rough impasto, the mottled and scurfed paint, sad testimony to his tutor's failing skills.

'Please,' says Mr Deller, 'do not believe the painting is unfinished. This . . .' (He points emphatically at a space above the canvas.) '. . . this is what I was *striving* for.' The old man begins to cough. Lifting both hands to his mouth, he gasps and hacks. William is alarmed to see his face turn crimson. Keeping well clear of his cough, he helps him back to his chair, where Mr Deller hawks at his feet a tawny, blood-flecked frogspawn. William studiously avoids the sight of it.

'When I went blind,' says Mr Deller, having recovered his breath, 'I agonised to understand the cause of it. Was it the black bile of errant imagination, as some physicians claim? What colour is my sputum?'

'Oh . . . it is difficult to tell.'

'No matter. Drawing and painting, Mr Stroud, are supposed to set dark humours to rights.'

'Indeed.'

'Perhaps . . .' Mr Deller blows through his teeth. He stirs and feebly fidgets in his chair. 'Perhaps I never worked hard enough to keep imbalance at bay.'

William frowns and rubs his fingertips together, as if to spark some understanding from them. He looks at the paintings sunk back in shadow. Twin Cynthias watch him from their tomb.

'That fifth canvas, Mr Deller . . . ?'

'My last work – which I have yet to show you – was my attempt to rescue her from the darkness.

I began it in haste and terror, the day after I ended my lessons with you.' A sudden weariness slows Mr Deller down. His eyelids droop, his head nods. William worries that he might be falling asleep – or worse. But Mr Deller's hands grip the rests of his chair and he speaks with his eyes closed, as though trained on some inner vision. 'Grief overtook me. I lost my purpose before I lost my sight. In the little time I had left I neglected the canvas for despair of ever fixing what I believed belonged there. Now, when it is too late, my eyes run riot in my head. The black bile in my system goes unpurged, my fancy unmastered. What remedies I had at my disposal, before the melancholy cloud fell, have been snatched from me.'

'Forgive me, sir. What remedies?'

Mr Deller's eyes open. William is seized by a spasm of fright at their icy indignation. 'Why, *work*, of course. What was the motto of Apelles? *Nulle dies sine linea*.'

'No day without a line.'

'A painter is most alive at his work. All other times, when he is attending to the body's needs, are more like sleep. So to be cut off from one's art – as I am by blindness, as *you* have been too long, William – is to waste one's life in a kind of enchantment.'

Mr Deller licks his lips. He begins to speak, for the first time, about his blindness.

'At night I dreamed of heavy clouds that seemed to drop upon me. Such oppression weighted my spirits that I feared them premonitions. And at length the fog began to settle on my days. I would be startled by a spot at the edge of my vision. I would turn my eyes in pursuit of it but could not catch the apparition. It stole upon me with the stealth of a hunter. Each dawn I awoke and less of the cloud lifted. It was like suffocation. I could not escape to breathe clearly; as if the vapours climbed from some chasm in my being . . .'

Mr Deller presses against the back of his chair. He is ashen faced and fading. William must do something.

'May I see the portrait, sir? Of your wife?'

Scolding himself for his pity, which will lumber him with an impossible task, William returns to the gaping hole and recovers the last, shrouded canvas. It is not big, perhaps twenty inches by twelve. Returning to his stool, he rests it on his lap, not daring to remove the cloth. Does the old man sense William's hesitation? Perhaps he too must steel himself before the unveiling of that sainted object.

'I landed,' says Mr Deller, in his manner of pursuing a thought that others are supposed to follow, 'in Amsterdam in the month of June 1642. I found, after some confusion, the house of Nicolaes Keyser – the man who was to be my tutor – near the Rozengracht.

My host was not at home. His manservant, who mercifully had learned some English from his master, opened the door to me and I learned that Heer Keyser was attending a funeral at the Oude Kerk. They were burying Saskia van Uylenburgh, the wife of Rembrandt van Rijn . . . You know who I am talking of?'

William bridles at this. 'Of course,' he says.

'In later years, once I had learned Dutch and ceased to be a stripling in his eyes, my tutor told me about Rembrandt's behaviour at the interment. He was distraught beyond decorum. Ragged with sorrow. Barely was his wife buried before he told the mourners of his desire to return home and *paint her.*'

'And,' says William, 'was it so for you?'

The old man shakes his head. '*Ingenium* abandoned me. When she died I seemed to lose all my faculties of conception. I was able to complete one grand and pompous commission, an allegory of Peace and Plenty, though my heart was a broken vessel. I still had a household, and now a child, to maintain. So I reconciled myself to the fancies of a new age. I produced, according to convention, all the poses and polish required of me. It was not for me – not then, as a courtier to the new King – to change painting in England. So you see the measure of the man before you. Rembrandt, robbed of his beloved, sought consolation in art. I found only artifice . . . Look at it now, my boy.'

Carefully, as though the object beneath were made of ashes, a carbon block that rough treatment would smash to cinders, William removes the woollen cloth.

'Can you see her clearly? What do you see?'

O God. How little he was able to set down! There is gathered splendour of an ancient oak, a few leaves precisely rendered in the foliage and the knotted trunk furrowed in brown ink. Vague premonitions of a garden – the blots and blurs of topiary, dark smudges of yew – precede a cursory square, a featureless shape that might be the manor. These background touches are washed in bistre and sepia. But black Indian ink, applied with a reed pen, is used for the foreground figure: an English Madonna seated in the oak tree's shade. Her voluminous dress is faintly limned, with one patch showing a pattern of embroidered flowers that William recognises from Cynthia's wardrobe.

The woman's face is a perfect blank.

'Mr Stroud, tell me what you see.'

'The outline of a young woman sitting on the grass in a garden. An oak tree, box hedges and yew – a landscape of civility and order. In the distance, on the right, this house.'

'What else?'

'She holds . . . what look like flowers.'

'*Above* the flowers?'

'Um . . . she is . . . large with child.'

The two men sit back in silence. The house shivers in the grip of the wind, its timbers creaking.

'The flowers in the portrait, William . . . May I call you William?'

'As you used to, sir.'

'The flowers are eyebright.' William, hearing an allusion but uncertain of it, gives no reply. 'A balm for the eyes. Belinda to mine, at the end of each day. My *Ooghen-troost.*'

William looks again at the vague flowers and at the floral design on Belinda's dress. He knows the conventional meaning of the bloom in portraiture. It signifies fidelity until death.

'The flowers are closed. You know what that means.'

'That the subject has departed.' William has been admitted to the secret chamber. His eyes have profaned the ghostly, unfinished image. Must he now play the necromancer and try to retrieve her from the shades? 'Mr Deller, you must understand that I remain far from any mastery of my craft.'

'There is native talent, sir.'

'And ignorance.'

'Do you doubt yourself?'

'Naturally.'

'Would you overcome that doubt?'

'If it were possible.'

'Then you must be tested to your limits.'

'Sir, as you know, I have not enjoyed the opportunities afforded other painters. With the exception of your teaching – for which I shall always be most grateful – I have benefited from no formal training.'

'That causes me no concern.'

'Perhaps it should.' William draws breath to dispel his nausea. He knows, before he speaks again, that conditional language will only deepen his obligation. 'Mr Deller, supposing I do accept this commission . . . how do you know I will succeed? I mean to say, if I fail, by what means will you recognise the failure?'

'I have nothing but faith. And hope that God will not abandon his servant. With my fingers for eyes I shall endeavour to sketch her features. With my mind's eye I shall try to describe her to you. I shall draw to my aid every sense I still possess.' The old man's face grows new folds: valleys of darkness and doubt. 'I have endured much, William. Oh, less than many, granted. But you will allow, there is no affliction so degrading for a man than to lose the one potency, the one purpose, for which he had been born and to the fulfilment of which – believing himself directed by his Creator – he has striven throughout his days. Such a scourge, indeed, so apt in its cruelty, that one might discern a higher design behind its visitation. It is the punishment I must endure . . .'

'Punishment? Whatever for?'

The old man grimaces. 'For what survival has required of me.'

1660

With senses recovered from the storm, Thomas Digby explores the fragrances in the house. Though customarily clogged by the stink of Lambeth, his apothecary's nose discerns particular plants: dittany and lavender and rosemary. He searches for and finds, while chewing his host's bread, parcels of dried flowers hanging from the rafters and others attached, with festive gaiety, to the overmantel of the hearth. Digby reads into these flowers what he has seldom known: the gentleness of a woman's touch. He licks his glove-flavoured fingers and gazes, empty headed, at the fresh primroses on the table.

'Feeling better?'

'Thank you.'

Before Digby can refuse, Nathaniel has refilled his goblet. The hospitality seems forced. Without his asking for food and this spiced stuff, it has been imposed upon him – each kindness a brisk necessity to disguise his host's impatience. 'Where do you do your painting?' Digby feels obliged to ask.

'I have a workroom that faces south. Would you care to see it?'

The man must be humoured; and Digby is not incurious. He forbids himself a longing glance at the ham, though hunger continues to roll about his belly. 'I should like that.'

They rise together, taking their goblets, and pock-faced Lizzie emerges from shadow to clear the table. In Nathaniel's wake, Digby catches a whiff of Turkish rosewater.

Leaving the hall and its congenial fire, they travel down a long, stone-floored corridor lit only by their candles. Digby hears the rain lashing against unseen windows. He wonders what lies beyond those closed doors. So much space: enough for a dozen of his Lambeth poor.

'Here it is.' Nathaniel entrusts his goblet to Digby and extracts a bunch of keys from his overall. 'A moment,' he says before slipping into the unlocked room. Digby waits, nestling the second goblet in the crook of his arm, and douses by mental effort his smouldering irritation; or is it envy of Nathaniel's happy lot? Just as impatience begins to make his knees tremble, the door, which has been left ajar, swings open and he is invited inside.

Candles in branches, young flames still hatching on their wicks, illuminate a cluttered workroom. There are several paintings, at varying stages of completion, propped against a far wall, and neither tapestries nor silk satin draperies: only whitewashed stone, the better to capture the light of day. Nathaniel, taking back his spiced wine, strides to the centre of the great room and smiles, his free hand on his hip.

'It is like a factory,' says Digby, meaning well.

'No, my house in London is the factory. This is an artisan's shop, where I pursue less urgent commissions.'

Pressing his goblet to his lips, Digby takes in the standing easel and the nails hammered into the wall, from which palettes hang like ancestral shields in a nobleman's castle. The palettes are stained with gobs of colour. Digby sees, without knowing their names, smears of ochre and red lake and vermilion; he lifts, with his little finger, a greasy membrane from a pot and peers at lead white.

'Unadulterated,' says Nathaniel, 'for light spots in the eyes.'

There is here something of the bawdy house, thinks Digby, wrinkling his nose at a collection of greasy and paint-stained rags. Approaching the large canvas on the easel, he smells linseed oil and goat glue; he sees papers scattered like leaves of a giant tree, and paintbrushes upside down in pots, their bristles exposed like upturned roots. Nathaniel, reading his trajectory, lights a lantern and sets it on a bench beside the easel.

'You drew a picture of me once,' says Digby.

'Indeed. Now this . . .'

'Do you have it still? That picture?'

Nathaniel's smile dwindles. He looks away from Digby's enquiring and a smut in his eye makes him blink. 'Amongst all my papers,' he says, 'after ten years?'

'Perhaps you rescued it.'

'I should . . . I should think it is somewhere. Now *here*,' says Nathaniel, raising his lantern to light the canvas, 'is my grandest project of the moment. You will see better tomorrow, of course. These brands do nothing justice.'

Digby looks at the painting. He ignores the vermilion drapery, the beautiful silks and perfect rendering of gleaming fruits. 'It's indecent,' he says.

'You are frank. It is a commission from the Earl of Surrey: a man of great culture.'

'Who are the doxies?'

'The nine Muses. This fair maiden is Peace and beside her the ample matron is Plenty.'

'What's she doing to her dugs?'

'Squeezing them for milk. The cherubs, you see, Plenty's offspring, catch the drops on their tongues. You do not approve.'

Digby must temper his reaction. Shaking his head like a drayhorse, he points at details and blusters. 'It is all very artfully done . . .'

'Plenty is my Lady Surrey. At least, she has my lady's *face*. Peace is her daughter, though I have omitted the second of her several chins.' Digby snorts and Nathaniel licenses his laughter with his own. 'I know,' he says. 'We cannot hope to reach the sitters as they are, only as they wish to be seen.'

'This is not the sort of painting I expected of you.' Digby feels his mind heavy, his tongue thick with uncertainty. He does not have the language to speak of these things.

'It is what is called for,' says Nathaniel. 'I am happy with the composition. Of course I can foresee your objections. What was it Winstanley wrote? "Speak nothing by imagination." That is too absolute. By imagination we bring new worlds into being.'

'Nature as it *is*, that was your code.' Ten years ago, thinks Digby, there was roughness in his drawings. What is all this gloss and flummery? 'I knew you when you were restless. A vagabond painter, you called yourself.'

'That was mockery . . .' Nathaniel shrugs and pulls the hempen apron over his head. He sheds his artisan disguises for the billowing shirt and leather breeches of a country squire. 'Constant movement is the enemy of Art. One needs stillness and equanimity in order to paint.'

Digby bears up to this polite rebuke. He wonders what could drive an earl to whore his wife and

45

daughter to a stranger's gaze. 'Will he give it to the King?'

'Pardon?'

'Your Earl of Surrey. As a gift to win favour.'

Nathaniel's expression darkens. He snatches the lantern and turns from the canvas, robbing it of colour. 'I have not had the effrontery to ask what he intends for the work. When you sell your coloured water, is it any concern of yours who drinks it?'

Digby feels his anger rise; he chokes it down, forcing the choler into his fists. Nathaniel has moved to another canvas and begins with his fingernail to scratch at something on its surface. Digby drains his goblet to the dregs and, wiping his mouth on his sleeve, hastens to compliment his host for his un-doubted talents. He admires resolutely two small portraits: one of a sea captain, ruddy cheeked in naval sash, standing before a swollen sea and tumid clouds, the other depicting a pretty dimpled maid resting on a gate. 'There is real life in these people,' he says. 'I should not be surprised to hear them speak.'

'Thank you.'

But Digby knows he has no feelings for art. He is a practical fellow. 'Do you have assistants in London?'

Nathaniel rubs his heavy jaw. He seems to bristle at the question. 'I do most of the painting. I will not entrust to Gaspars and Buckshorns the tedium of silk and draperies.'

'I meant no offence.'

Perhaps sensing his churlishness, Nathaniel wipes his fingers on a strip of linen. 'My dear Thomas, you caused none. Do you smoke?'

The rain having eased, the men lean together at the open casement, each lighting his pipe with a taper. It is finest Virginia tobacco. Digby considers making a connection with his deeper purpose but courage fails him. 'In all honesty, Nathaniel.' He clears his throat and swallows. 'Might you not profit from the King's restoration?'

Nathaniel sucks pensively. His pipe seethes and whistles, the red glow illuminating his brow. 'In my profession, perhaps. Do not be angry – though I had employment, I found only disappointment in the Commonwealth.'

'Amen.'

'The land's only value was the revenue it brought. The fashion for plainness was no more honest than the fashion for ornament it replaced. The art I dreamed of could not grow there.'

'That sounds like a complaint, yet you enjoy worldly success.'

The barb in Digby's voice lights coals of anger in the painter. 'They sold the dead King's art collection. You never saw it. *I* saw it. Such treasures lost. So much for your "triumphant" republic.'

'It was not mine, you know.' Digby feels the path

of their discourse slipping beneath them; yet he cannot sugar his words. 'The sale of those treasures was a small matter for the people, since none but kings and courtiers were ever permitted to *see* them.'

'The revenue never reached your poor, your needy. It went to pay the King's creditors.'

This is froth and Digby says so. 'What have such vanities to do with life?'

'They are the gilt that remains when we are decayed.' Nathaniel puffs angrily, scowling at the turbulent sky. Well, thinks Digby, he was ever given to this useless passion. Humour him. You have need of his friendship.

'No doubt,' he concedes, 'you are right. And I am a very heathen in matters of art.'

On the way back to the fragrant hall, there to discuss the reasons for Digby's visit, their conversation harries the sleeping manor. Drink and forced jollity have made them loud: their voices chase like the spirits of hollering children up the stairway to the landing.

'Ever think about the colony? Do you?' Digby points at Nathaniel's nose. 'I remember when you arrived – we were clearing furze. You looked so out of place and so eager to please. Your hands were shaking.'

'You noticed that?'

'Painters are not alone in having eyes.' With insincere mirth, Digby laughs. 'You howled when we felled that oak.'

'*We?* You played no part in it, as I recall.'

'Well, but I had to dissuade you from protesting. A lifeless thing . . .'

'Not lifeless. It was six hundred years old, from the rings of grain.'

'And how would you know that . . .' (Stop swinging from the banister, Digby's sergeant-master conscience orders. You are behaving like an ape.) '. . . how would you have known if we had not cut it down?'

'They did it because it belonged to the King.'

Digby shakes his head, trying to speak calmly. 'It was nothing so subtle,' he says.

Something catches Nathaniel's attention. He looks abruptly up the stairway, into the throat of the darkness. Digby sees him reach for the handrail, his face transfigured by concern, and follows the direction of his gaze.

A young woman is standing on the stairhead, her legs concealed by a white shift and a fur gown draped about her shoulders. She carries no candle or taper; her appearance was heralded by no sound. Digby steps back, raising his hand level with his ear but stopping short of removing a phantom hat.

'Husband? We have a guest?'

Nathaniel ascends three steps, lifting his lantern to illuminate the stairs and his wife. The face, which Digby discerns, is round and full lipped; her long black hair is worn loose, with strands awry from a recently vacated pillow. Digby swallows a hard knot in his throat.

'Oh, Belinda. You should be sleeping.' Nathaniel turns to Digby, his cheeks flushed. 'She should be sleeping . . .' He climbs the stairs to assist her. 'In your condition. Let me help you . . .'

Belinda Deller offers a pale hand to her husband. With his other arm he reaches about her waist to guide her down the stairs, while Belinda carries his lantern. Digby hears them whispering.

'*I trust I am not improperly dressed.*'

'*Well, um – we are not alone.*'

'*You surprise me.*'

Digby hears gentle mockery in the lady's voice, and more humble, Kentish inflections. He does not know where or how to stand. Should he offer to help, or stay put in the hallway? The couple is descending now. He sees Belinda's heaviness. Without embarrassment she smiles at him. 'I am almost down,' she says. 'Oh, Nathaniel, do not fuss.'

'The last step . . . there.'

Digby has rarely seen such unblemished skin, its pallor unpoisoned by ceruse. She wears none of the curl-papers one might expect on a somnolent lady;

yet she is, in her plainness, so becoming that he must look away momentarily.

'How do you do, sir?'

'Madam.' Digby performs a reverence that might not look amiss from a St James's Park fop.

'Forgive me,' blusters Nathaniel. 'This is my wife, Belinda. My heir also – though he has yet to show himself. My dear, may I introduce Thomas Digby?'

She wears a wry smile, not ungenerous, that makes a single crease on her left cheek, just below the nose. Digby drifts towards her eyes. They are large and black and swollen.

'Are you an artist, Mr Digby?'

'Me? No.'

'Mr Digby was a friend in my youth . . .'

'We were Diggers together. On St George's Hill. And then . . . afterwards.'

Belinda's expression does not falter; but her smiling eyes lose some of their light. Nathaniel, lacking his wife's diplomacy, fumbles for her hand. 'My dear, you are disobeying the doctor's instructions.'

'The doctor thinks childbearing an illness, Mr Digby: to be slept off like a fever.'

Nathaniel looks flustered. It is a strange manifestation of uxoriousness, this desire to have her restored to her bed. Digby wonders whether Deller might be jealous of another man's gaze. Or else, and this chills him for being more likely, he is ashamed of what Digby represents.

'Come, to bed with you. Where is Bathsheba?'

'Snoring like all Seven Sleepers in one. You are most welcome to our house, Mr Digby. I hope I shall make your acquaintance properly in the morning.'

'Of course.'

'Shall I accompany you?'

'No need.' She brushes Nathaniel's shoulder gently. 'How far have I to go?' Belinda takes possession of her husband's lantern and ascends with it to her chamber. Digby looks at his fingernails, hearing only the susurration of her nightdress and seeing, in the rapt corner of his vision, her white hand as it skips along the handrail. Nathaniel follows in her wake, as though afraid she might fall.

'Goodnight, gentlemen.'

'Goodnight, madam,' says Digby. He looks up but sees only Nathaniel halfway up the staircase, leaning forward to be certain of her progress.

'Be careful of the flame.'

Digby hears Belinda laugh; then the opening and closing of a door. Nathaniel comes heavily back down the stairs. 'My wife is a headstrong woman,' he says. 'And impatient of ceremony.'

'Congratulations.'

'I grant it is a late age to begin a family.' Digby protests that they are not so old but Nathaniel ignores him. 'I sacrificed my prime to painting. It was my sole mistress. For many years I thought such things as love – and comfort with another being – were forbidden to me.'

This must be false, thinks Digby. No man, unless he is a saint, can sublimate his will so entirely. Nathaniel will have found warm bodies to press while his paint was drying. Digby remembers one, on the common, whom his host had lightly toyed with.

'But it was too sterile a life. And sterility began to infect my paintings . . .'

'You married her, then, for your art's sake?'

Nathaniel's gaze is not affronted. 'For love,' he replies. 'Believe it. When Belinda accepted my proposal I felt like one of God's elect – if you will pardon the expression.'

Digby pardons it. He walks pensively with his host back towards the great hall. He has no wife and child, though perhaps a bastard somewhere. Occasionally, sitting at the window of his shop, his hands weary from working the pestle, he will watch street children at their games, or conspiring to steal apples from a tradesman's stall. He cannot despise them for their dirt and mischief, though they would rob him of everything given half a chance. Many citizens mutter darkly against these human vermin. He has watched prentice boys celebrate with small beer their latest skirmish against them. What if *his* son were among the children beaten? Is his daughter one of those scrawny whores to whom, his face averted for fear of temptation, he sometimes slips a charitable token?

They enter the hall and regain their seats at the table. Digby is disappointed to find the ham gone and the bread also. His host is smiling, his hands folded on his complacent belly. 'By women's eyes this doctrine I derive: they sparkle still the right Promethean fire. They are the arts, the academes . . .' Vaguely he trails off, the words (whosesoever they be) eluding him. He looks at Digby and laughs apologetically.

'She is . . . uh . . . very graceful.'

'At first I was enchanted, like a love-struck schoolboy. I felt young again.' Nathaniel stops abruptly. 'Have *you* a—?'

'No, I live alone.' Only Samuel, his apprentice, for company: a sullen lad, homesick for his parents and Warwickshire, no spark but a diligent worker. He cannot be taken to America without his father's consent. Digby will have to abandon him in Lambeth. He foresees this betrayal with dismay. 'Do you show your work to your wife?' he asks.

'She has an excellent eye, and other qualities besides. She has, you know, the healing gift. Like *you*. She knows the properties of all the medicinal plants in our herb garden . . .'

How gulled can a lover be? Doubtless she consults an almanac.

'She has become my helpmeet and companion. It is a love match, for she brought a meagre dowry. I intend that our son will have the same freedom to marry whomsoever he wishes.'

Digby is tiring of these happy musings. He wonders when the child is due and shudders to think of the hooks and thimbles that a Lambeth midwife uses. Still, in the country her chances will be better.

Nathaniel reaches across the table for the jug of wine. His fingers taste the sides for warmth and he abandons his intent. 'But forgive me,' he says. 'I have yet to learn about *your* life in the years since we parted.'

So it begins. Digby would like to have a flagon of ale to help him through. 'You told me,' he says, 'in your last letter what things *they* did to you.' Nathaniel's head and body grow rigid. His jaw is violently set on the suppression of movement. 'How you were arrested on the hill and interrogated.'

'It was not . . . It was not so severe,' says Nathaniel.

'And you were dismissed with a token whipping.' Digby sees the distress he is causing. Perhaps it is unwise to raise the spectre of Nathaniel's humiliation. Yet he must be reminded of his suffering if their old friendship is to be rekindled. 'As for me, I was imprisoned for a month. I dared not tell you in my letters how, on my release, I wanted to join the Digger colonies in the Midlands. But I was under watch as a troublemaker, so I had to stay in Lambeth. For a time I dreamed of piracy in the Corsair Republic. Oh, I know what you would say. But consider, Nathaniel. No tenancy, no enclosures, no absolute power of one man over another. Pirates at sea live more freely than Englishmen on land.'

'But without justice.'

'I forget what that word means.'

Nathaniel rubs his lips with his forefinger. Digby remembers this nervous gesture: seeing it fills him with sorrow.

'For years I lived in near-despair. I consulted the Bible . . .' Digby's voice strains, the cords in his throat tighten. Damn this wine: it has made him maudlin. 'I opened the Bible but could find no meaning where my finger fell. I found myself unguided. Truly I believed, with the war's end and the King's beheading, that a new age was dawning. God's justice seemed at hand . . . But we were scattered and the rich man crowed from his dunghill.'

Nathaniel rises from his back-stool. Digby senses, though his face is buried in his hands, the painter crouching beside him. There is a sonorous crack from his bending knees. 'Hope does not live in the head,' says Nathaniel. 'If hope were built on reason we should all despair. It is a product of the soul, a condition of being, immune to the state of the world—'

'Which is corrupted.'

'Which is corrupted but *may*, by the will of God, return to the paradise our first parents knew.'

Digby withdraws his hands from his face. He would not have Nathaniel read this as agreement and so sours his complexion with a sneer. 'You have read too much complacent literature,' he says. 'Let solace come through fancy, through sweet soft words. We must build a fortress for liberty. Even to hope in England now is to fail. And Providence will not reward us for sitting on our arses.'

Nathaniel's knees creak again with his rising. He retreats from this dalliance with philosophy, offended perhaps by coarse language. Digby must be more careful.

'England is lost. She is sinking back into her old iniquities. Impiety is rife. Courtiers are returning from the Continent in French frippery. There's even talk of reopening the *theatres*, God help us. Then there's a new settlement to face. What fate awaits signatories to the old King's death one can too easily imagine. Less clear is the future for principled dissenters.'

'What do you intend to do, then?'

'Set sail for the colonies. *America*. Think of it, friend. Virgin territory – a land without history, without boundaries. We would not be the first to escape hostility in this way . . .'

'*We*, Thomas?'

Digby guffaws. He has outpaced himself. 'I am not proposing to go *alone*. I warrant you, one can be a hermit in England.'

'Who do you expect to go with?'

'Those who were with us on the common.'

'The Diggers? Do you know where they are now?'

'Some. We will find them.'

'How?'

'By the grace of God. Because we cannot but follow our destiny. You have not forgotten what we achieved there – on the hill and in Cobham? What we touched upon. Equality on *Earth* as in Heaven.'

'Fine ideals, Thomas. Long ago.'

'Ideals are timeless.' Digby will not be discouraged. He expected resistance. What must the Apostles have felt when they were told to leave their wives and children? 'You know,' he continues, 'since you lived there, what life is like in Lambeth. Without work, men are as good as dead, and with work they are no better than turnspit dogs, running to no gain.'

'Well, it is not so for you.'

'It is not *my* condition which angers me.' Something glints in Nathaniel's eye which compels Digby to insist. 'Truly. I am fortunate to have my profession. I could have been a tanner, wrist deep in dog turds and stale . . .'

'Your skills are valuable to your less fortunate fellows.'

Digby smiles sourly. 'With my coloured water?'

Each man needs to persuade the other. Nathaniel presses his point with his knuckles on the table. 'I watched you treat the sick on the common. That teething infant . . .'

'She died.'

'But your kindness eased her passing.'

Digby cannot stand the heat of Nathaniel's conviction; or is it desire for the same? 'I wish that I believed you, friend.' He thinks for a moment, chewing his thumb. He finds another avenue for persuasion. 'At least she died an innocent. The same cannot be said for adults in Lambeth. Every day, the number of paupers grows. Countless live as beggars, they throw themselves on the parish and the parish cannot help them. So in desperation they steal, turn footpad, cut throats. The women swive for bread.'

'But this is not *your* burden . . .'

Digby pretends he did not hear. 'It is impossible in a city to revive our old ways. With two friends I try to assist souls as well as bodies. But the people have forgotten what they mean to God, they are so lumpen and reconciled to their baseness.' Now, *now*, must he press home his advantage. Digby ignores the signals that ought to discourage him. This is Nat Deller, his brother of old, who shared his rations amid the flowering gorse, who painted the faces of children and sang so sweetly, to the Diggers' delight, when they sat beneath the cold stars. Surely he can still win him over. If God intends it, he will rescue all those who have wandered from the Truth. 'This is why we must leave England. In the New World, who is to say that Grace may not flow where now stands corruption?'

Nathaniel seems to deflect these words, standing large and opaque like a mountain. Digby's bowels ache with despair. The man is immovable.

'Charles Stuart seems a more reasonable man than his father.'

'Oh, do not believe it! In the days to come we can expect only iniquity and unrighteousness. The King may tyrannise over men but he will answer to Christ, the world's great leveller.'

Nathaniel's head jerks. On a reflex he glances across his shoulder, and Digby wonders whether there is not a royalist spy hiding behind a tapestry.

'At least,' Nathaniel says with slow deliberation, 'the return of the King is preferable to these late disorders of the state.' He quells the coming protest with a raised, open hand: a gesture that Digby imagines Christ making to still the waters. 'I cannot come with you to America. Do you not see that? It is not my path.'

'It is an Englishman's duty to bring Salvation to the New World. Did we not fight the antichristian party in the war?'

'I did not fight,' says Nathaniel. 'I sketched and painted.'

Digby stares at the candles until his eyeballs ache. Unthinkingly, he rips a petal from a primrose and sets about shredding it. 'Very well,' he says, 'if I cannot persuade you to come in person . . .'

'What?'

'Perhaps you might contribute to the costs of the expedition.' Nathaniel says nothing. He steers the bowl of primroses out of Digby's reach. 'Or have you spent all your wealth on becoming a complete gentleman?'

'A complete gentleman,' says Nathaniel, 'who is your host.'

'I did not know what to expect when I rode here. You think you still possess God's favour.'

'I would not presume.'

'Even so, I can see it in your eyes. Do not become too accustomed to your comfort. God will punish us for our failings.'

'God, I fear, will punish me more if I neglect the gift He gave me. Others may have other callings but I know mine and it is here. In England.' Nathaniel sits on the table, most indecorously close to Digby's shoulder. Digby's blood freezes to feel a sympathetic hand on his arm. 'There is no destination save the grave. In life we have perpetual seeking, with moments of rest – in love's haven, or fleeting sleep. When we think we have reached the final ground of our searching, we find the soil shifts and unravels beneath us. I do not believe that we can build a lasting mansion on earth.'

Digby says nothing. This, he thinks, is comfort speaking.

'Perhaps in art,' says Nathaniel.

'What?'

'One may seek perfection. In my paintings, Time – which makes us contradict ourselves – is stilled.'

'On canvas,' says Digby, sneering, 'which is without life.'

Nathaniel sighs and moves away to prod the burning logs. Digby watches him bitterly. 'The test of spiritual value is in community. Your seclusion here is ungodly.'

'It failed, Thomas.'

'We were given no chance! They hounded us from the hill, they beat us in Cobham, and when the gentry's hand failed, the army finished us off. You were *there*. You saw *this* happen.' He points to a scar barely visible on his chin. Only the reddening of his face shows up its ivory.

'Vice has ever been the fruit of power. Virtue, redemption, love – these exist only in private.'

'Reputation, ease, licence! Call them, Mr Deller, by their proper names!' Digby knows that he has failed, wretchedly failed, to sway the man.

'I see no advantage in continuing this debate. I cannot have sedition under my roof.' Nathaniel is going: he is slipping away from all persuasion. 'I shall instruct my man to equip you for the night.'

'So you will walk away,' Digby scoffs. Anger with himself chooses the straighter channel. 'That a man of principle, my friend, should turn tail and flee. You're no better than the peasants. They would cheer to see the royal mount shit.'

'Thomas, my hospitality has its limits.'

'Am I to declare the King's nag above shitting? What, then – does it transubstantiate hay? Should I perhaps make idols of His Majesty's pack-hounds?'

'Mr Digby! Your anger does not justify obscenity. And your principles sound to me more akin to bile than ardent choler . . . I wish you well. I will pray for the success of your venture. But I will not come with you.'

'Nathaniel – you once did call me brother.'

'Then take some fraternal advice. Learn to curb your anger and your tongue. They will serve the paupers whom you disdain no advantage, and they may well destroy you.'

'I disdain no one.'

'They have disappointed you.'

Nathaniel rings the handbell. Lizzie appears so swiftly, a phantom ruffling the candle flames, that Digby starts. She must have heard every word of his humiliation. He reads, in her bowed head and the pallor of her cheeks, that she is frightened.

'Wake up Frederick,' says her master, all kind consideration gone. 'Tell him Mr Digby will be our guest for the night.'

'Very good, sir.'

'You will not wake that old man?'

'It is his duty,' says Nathaniel impatiently. He sniffs and pats his sides. There are bruises of tiredness under his eyes that Digby has not noticed before. 'We will speak again tomorrow. In daylight this dispute will seem less terrible.' They wait apart: Nathaniel wearily slouching in the doorway, Thomas like a scolded schoolboy confined to his stool. 'Goodnight, Mr Digby.'

'Sleep well . . . Mr Deller.'

1680

Tonight, as many nights since her father's blindness, Cynthia is summoned to the kitchen window by the hooting of tawny owls. Opening the casement gently, not to startle the birds that may be near, she bathes her face in the cool darkness. That forlorn note again; and in memory she is lying in her childhood bed, her father at work near by. (She can see a sliver of light beneath her door; she hears the chiming of brushes washed in a glass. When the owl cries she calls out for comfort. Her nurse's nightdress is rumpled and malodorous. There is no solace in it.) Now, far off, in the wooded vale before a barren hillside, a second bird replies. All of the garden so darkly poised – the vague topiary and crumbling walls, the limes and ash trees under their summer burden – seems bewitched by that melancholy song. Can it be called a song? The poet is mistaken who writes *Tu-whit, to-who*. That is two owls in conversation. To prove her theory, the near owl hoots again, from the hollow of a rambling oak that, as a child misreading beetle holes, she called the fairy tree. The garden holds this oak, this unseen bird, in the palm of its hand. Cynthia covers her candle with a dish the better to conceal herself. A ruffling sound, very near, makes her look into the flower bed. Rats, or mice, stirring beneath the rank nettles. From somewhere beside the clogged lake a copulating vixen shrieks. Cynthia shuts the casement and returns to her seat.

William Stroud's coat is draped across the strut of a chair and she resists the impulse to brush, from its leather surface, dried crusts of mud and clay. She wonders, can it still be warm? Is it imbued with him? His riding hat she caresses as though it were a somnolent cat on the table. She pictures him upstairs, at this instant, speaking with her father, while she must make do with his empty garments.

Cynthia presses a hand on her stomach. There is a ball of tension, from compression of breath, that her whalebone busk only amplifies. She is sorry now that she woke Lizzie to help her fasten it. How completely she gave herself away, blushing with excitement while the maid pulled and pretended not to notice the shortness of her breath. With quick fingers Cynthia checks, for a third time, the sugar cakes on their pewter dish, the cleanliness of the glasses and the quantity of sherry sack in the bottle . . .

William almost touched her outside her father's chamber. She saw his hand come near and then abandon its intent. Thank Heaven and alas, she managed to conceal her fright.

She has waited long enough, tonight as always. She sorts among her pots for the boxwood comb that she brought down before William's arrival. She does her best, lacking both mirror and maid, to restore some life to her stale ringlets. She palpates her topknot and feels it coming loose, like the laurels growing wild in the garden. It is all vanity. The stove bubbles and snores. A deep weariness threatens to overwhelm her. She rests with her hands on the kitchen table. When she has recovered and the spinning air has stilled about her head, she gathers up her loaded tray and climbs the servants' staircase, careful not to trip or spill anything.

There is a long, creaking corridor, deafening in its emptiness, for her to negotiate, in near obscurity, before she reaches her father's door. She knocks, raising one knee in most unladylike fashion to steady the tray. She hears susurration within, as though she were disturbing an arcane sect at its oblations. They are tidying away their altar, secreting their chalices and censers. Cynthia cannot keep from smiling to hear her father's hissed instructions and the furtive movements of William Stroud obeying.

'A moment,' he calls. She waits for the covering up of the numinous, forbidden object; then enters to find William stepping back from a shrouded canvas, her father seated with a stubborn and comical expression of innocence. *There it is*, she thinks, scrupulously avoiding the canvas with her gaze. She asserts placid neutrality over her features as she sets down the tray. What universal feigning in this little room. William, who has retreated to his stool, watches her bent back as she pours the sherry. She senses his regard, not icy like a stranger's on her nape, but warm as his breath. She must be careful not to spill the drink.

'Your garden . . .' William Stroud clears his throat. 'You wanted to work it into the painting?'

'*Hortus conclusus*. In time of crisis, or discord, the garden means order, peace, abundance. It was a kind of refuge to me from the world's madness.' Cynthia, without saying a word, finds her father's staring, vacant hands and raises them to his plate of sugar cakes. She hopes he will eat. For weeks his appetite has been failing; he complains that all food sickens him. The *kandeel*, the Dutch biscuits, indulgence of his taste for sweet things are her attempt to keep him in this world. 'Thank you, my dear.'

'I'm setting the glass before you.'

'Put it in my hand. I will eat the cake later.'

'You promise to, Father?'

He is immediately angered. With ill-tempered claws he shakes her away and Cynthia resignedly takes the plate from him, replacing it with the glass. Mr Deller seems to listen to the echo of his petulance, his undignified temper. Is it shame that distorts his mouth, or the liquid flame of the sherry?

'My garden,' he continues. 'My wife loved it. I used to paint, often, or sketch for my pleasure, its unruly limes and ordered beds. There is a bower where the very shade is green. Paradise, you know, is a garden. We used to walk in it, hearing the birds. Did we not, Cynthia?'

'On my arm.'

'Cynthia would describe things to me. A paradox worthy of Lancelot Andrewes. My daughter has my eyes and I have hers.'

William looks for the truth of this. It is difficult to tell from those frozen spheres. He tries to imagine what it would be never to see Cynthia's face; never again to know the fawnish freckles on her nose, or the unfashionable but to him entirely charming russet of her hair.

'It was a kind of consolation,' says Mr Deller. 'She had only to say what she saw and my memory supplied the vision. The garden is one thing that I will not leave to decay. I have kept my man at the task. Others in my employment I have, alas, been obliged to let go.'

'Father, if you have no further need of me . . .'

'You may go, Cynthia. I still have more to discuss with Mr Stroud.'

William rises to acknowledge her departure. He

has always found injurious the way that Deller speaks to her. At home, though his father has dominion of the mill, it is the women who lord it over the household.

'Goodnight, gentlemen.'

Leaving, Cynthia notices that the front of her skirt is pinned back. She meant to conceal this proof of her domestic chores. Now it is too late. She considers herself in the empty corridor: tired and dishevelled, a spinster maid. Her soul quakes; she is followed by the memory of William's eyes when she left the room. She shakes her head angrily. She should not believe what she thought she saw there.

William for his part listens for her footfalls. How can he sit munching like an ass when she is only yards away? It is a relief to hear her go. 'Mr Deller, you spoke before about punishment . . .'

'I did.'

'Might I ask what you meant by it?'

Mr Deller drains his glass, sherry dew gathering in his beard. He waits to be served again. 'I never confided in you, did I?'

The words are all the more intimate for their proximity as Wiliam fills the old man's glass. 'When . . . when I was your pupil?'

'There seemed no need. I could contain everything. It is a gentleman's task to keep hid things that are not welcome.'

As usual William struggles to follow. He returns, on tiptoe, to his seat.

'Now,' whispers Mr Deller, 'I am so leaky that I cannot . . .' His lips tighten almost to vanishing. He masters himself and continues. 'Wretched is he who is born fortunate, William.'

'For he shall inherit the earth?'

'And then lose it. I was born with every advantage, wealthy enough to pursue my course unchecked by need. I do not know how my father guessed my passion for art. Perhaps he saw the fire in my eyes.'

William grunts. His father has always been too busy to look into his.

'As a child, I spent hours enraptured in the contemplation of nature. The pulse that shapes a growing plant, the shadows cast by clouds on a hillside. And yet I was never at ease. I could not bear to take leave of the moment. To see nature's bounty was not enough: I had to capture something of its essence, preserve the flower's bloom before it bruised and withered.'

'Why did you study in Holland?'

'My father had had dealings with the House of Orange in Brabant. It was from that time he came to admire the Dutch Republic. And so it made sense that I was sent there instead of Rome. It was my father who found my tutor, Nicolaes Keyser. He had learned English from mercenaries who fought with him at 's-Hertogenbosch.'

'Was he a good teacher?'

'Better than I was a pupil. You may struggle to imagine, from this old husk, that I was once head-strong and ambitious. For a few years my restless spirit was occupied with learning. But I watched the merchant ships and their captains with envy.'

'You did not enjoy your work?'

'I wanted to apply it to the world. Ah . . . if I could tell that young fool what I know now. Stay put. Continue to learn. Above all, be patient: the world will not run away from you.' Mr Deller drinks; his fingers twitch above the sugar cakes then shrink back. 'Holland was remarkable. Such proliferation of pictures! In the markets and print shops, in the guildhalls. I do not pretend it was all great art. But I dreamed of such a culture for England. A country with paintings in every home: instead of which, Parliament sold off the dead King's art collection. What little we possessed we lost, so blithely.'

William pictures himself in Holland. Rembrandt van Rijn was a miller's son. Might not *his* skills be valued there? 'Did you finish your apprenticeship?'

'Civil war broke out in England. Tradesmen gossiped in the Exchange, rumours travelled on the canals. I could not stay away. So I sailed without my master's leave to Harwich. The first King Charles was not yet dead: that high summer of impossibilities lay four years off. I followed in Parliament's wake, sketching events for posterity, etching for pamphlets. And don't think I despised the work. On the contrary: it was preferable to the graft of copying in a garret, or filling in the edges of my master's handiwork. I had found a way of making my art *useful*. Ancillary to life, essential to it.'

'Essential how, sir?'

'I meant to document the world, so much of which – most indeed – is deemed unworthy of an artist's attention. Nature, according to convention, interests only as dead ornaments. And I hate a hunting scene with its rotting aftermath. The poor, meanwhile, are picturesque at best and unfit subjects for portraiture. There is beauty in everything that is made. Even a burned house, or a rain-soaked gallows, offers subtleties of colour and texture that *must* belong on canvas. That was . . . oh . . . my dream. To celebrate God's vision.'

'Did He envisage the gallows?'

'He gave us eyes that we might *use* them.'

William is surprised by the old man's vigour. If he were kept to this subject, Mr Deller might live to eighty. Yet already he is tiring. Time may be short and the confession (if such it is) continues.

'I lived for a time in London. Painters like Will Dobson could still find work in Oxford. But I was for Parliament and so moved to Lambeth in search of cheaper rent. I copied like a drudge and designed tapestries for Mortlake . . .' He breaks off. His wandering eyes settle on a phantom. Drink and memories extract him from William's company. It only lasts a moment but William shudders to watch, it reeks so of mortality. 'I was able,' says Mr Deller, 'to see some of the paintings that belonged to the King. I befriended one of the commissioners, and so ended my penury . . .'

William is confused. 'Forgive me – what commissioners?'

'Two of the buyers rewarded me for painting their portraits. Colonel Hutchinson and Colonel Webb. I would have done it in return for one of their meanest purchases. But the colonels had other plans. They did not buy those wonders for themselves. Instead, they sold them to Spain and France . . .'

Mr Deller's liver-spotted hand trembles as he drains his second glass. He brandishes the empty vessel, even shaking it to make his thirst clear. Looking down at the white beard stained with drink and the bald dome, wisped with meagre strands of hair, William must breathe through his mouth to escape a cankerous odour.

'Go on,' pipes the old man, perhaps sensing William's reluctance to replenish his glass. 'I must tell you something you may not know.'

'Yes?'

'I left London in disgust at the fate of the collection.

I had heard of a certain community newly formed in Surrey. I was, let us say, on conversant terms with radicals. So I followed them to a hill where they were undertaking this . . . experiment in just living.'

William sits up, intrigued. 'What were they? Ranters?'

'I lost contact with them.'

'Were they your friends?'

Mr Deller looks uncomfortable, as though troubled in his digestion. But he has eaten nothing. 'There was one young man. A very passionate fellow and absolute. I remember the fire in his eyes. A tremulous flame of enthusiasm which I could, with a word, extinguish or else rouse to conflagration.' William frowns and wonders who, precisely, the old man is recalling. Is it *himself*? 'I was scarcely his senior,' Mr Deller continues, 'and he was used to a life much harder than mine. Yet for some reason I felt almost a father to him. No, rather an uncle. I was never . . . I do not think I shared his expectations.'

'What became of him?'

'He wanted, after the King's return, to found a community in America.'

'Did he succeed?'

'He travelled to the Dutch Republics. For want, I presume, of followers. I received one letter from him.'

'And then?'

'He died fighting for the Dutch fleet. In the Med-way.'

William was still a boy when the Chatham fleet was destroyed. He had learned to despise as traitors those who took part on Holland's side. As though reading his thoughts, the old painter shakes his head. 'I would not presume to condemn him. He behaved as his conscience dictated.'

'Against his country?'

Mr Deller wipes imagined crumbs or dust from his chest. 'It seems,' he says, 'an age away.'

William, hoping to stave off sleep, crams a sugar cake into his mouth. He takes an infantile pleasure in behaving grossly. He nearly swoons with the tempta-tion to stick out his tongue.

'Are the jumbals good?'

'*Mm* . . .' William guiltily covers his mouth. 'Won't you try some?'

Mr Deller shudders at the very notion. William tells himself he must drink no more.

'May I continue my story?'

'Please.'

'After my experience in the country, I put all my hope in the Commonwealth. With my honest eye – as I thought it – surely I could prosper in the warts-and-all republic.'

'Did you meet Cromwell?'

'I was commissioned to paint his portrait for

foreign ambassadors. The Lord Protector seemed to me cold – convinced of his purpose. I never met the later, doubting man.'

On his only trip to London as a boy, with his father, to visit relatives who had survived both plague and fire, William had looked up from the shops of Westminster Hall to see the exhumed heads of Cromwell and his generals. (Posthumous punishment was a good way to limit bloodshed.) Nobody else seemed to notice them. But William gawped, first in horror and then in fascination, until his father growled, 'Enough, boy,' and pulled him angrily away.

'I was disappointed,' continues Deller. 'I wanted, though I knew not how, to establish a truly English art. A commonwealth of visible things, where all matter is worthy of contemplation. Alas, our new masters had no interest in such things: only property and the foundation of colonies abroad. I managed to find some work, not least from the Earl of Surrey. You know, I am sure, the importance of having a patron.'

William knows – only too well. He permits himself a third cake and munches mournfully.

'Then, about the time our Lord Protector died, my fortunes began to improve. I met my wife. She was the daughter of a glover in Maidstone. Such loveliness . . .' Mr Deller licks his lips but seems only to dry them. His raw tongue drags on the skin and he grimaces to swallow saliva. Again he drinks, and then gasps. William begins to fret about him.

'You inherited this house?'

'My brother Robert died most unexpectedly. Perhaps . . . perhaps beneath my sorrow, my worse angel allowed delight – treasonable, greedy delight – to enter in. I took possession of his wealth and *that* was why . . .' He stops and sniffs loudly. Wiping his nose with the back of his trembling hand, he smiles and William sees the decayed mouth, its snaggle-teeth. 'My daughter was born here, early in June. For a wetnurse we found a disgraced girl from the village whose child was stillborn. So there was hope for Cynthia at least.'

William would like to ask how Belinda died; he dares nothing, however, and from maudlin thoughts Mr Deller delivers them both with a laugh. 'I spent a decade painting for the court of Charles. Polish and gloss were called for, not gnarled honesty. Brilliant colours and uniform light. Paint smoothly applied, so that the surface of a canvas *gleamed* when you saw it obliquely. No obstructions or excrescences to snag the wanton eye.' He strokes an imagined chain on his chest – the symbol of royal patronage. 'My father was a patriot, opposed to court and its privileges. And yet within so few years of his death, I had changed our cloth entirely. I became a man of fashion . . .'

William cannot disapprove. Sometimes he lies

awake, with the snoring of his parents and the dogs from the next chamber, dreaming himself into a full-bottomed wig and embroidered coat 'after the Persian manner'. In truth he cares little for lace and plumes; but the status they confer would blow away for ever the chaff of his miller's life.

'Do not think them as fine as they appear.' Mr Deller's voice is beginning to sway. 'Costly clothes are mere disguises. I have known courtiers to shit in corners, in chimneys and coal-houses. They are all powdered periwigs and joyless smiles.' William watches his leering host. That 'shit' is the first coarse word he has ever heard him utter. 'Licence and lechery! I was called to paint our monarch's drabs. Very lovely they were – pert fruit, spiced oranges. I would have *bitten* . . .' He stops, panting, his glass listing in his lap. Gingerly, William rescues it and replaces it on the low table. Mr Deller's head lolls. His eyes are closed, his mouth open. William dithers, almost sitting on thin air. Should he make him eat a little to soak up the drink? He starts when Deller's sightless eyes open, by chance, on his face. 'I was a friend, you know, to Lely.'

'The painter?'

'The *manufacturer*. By the time I left London, he had formalised his poses into a numbered series. Can you conceive of such artifice? I was glad to come to this house on the downs.'

'It was to my profit,' says William.

'Hm? What?'

'That you retired, sir. Otherwise I would have known nothing—'

'I did not *retire* from painting.' Now why is he angry? William chews his lip. *Is* he angry? 'This is where I meant to achieve my earthly purpose. I would invent that English art, sprung from our native soil, imbued with the genius of the country.'

William looks back at the few surviving paintings: those dark interiors without embellishment or extraneous detail. So much for 'Nature': it all seems to take place in the head.

'I was beginning – just *beginning*, William – to approach my goal when my eyesight failed. After the light of inspiration has flared we are abandoned to darkness. Forsaken by our art, we fall into melancholy. When I was still painting, I could be alone with my work gladly. But to live in company when the work is gone is loneliness entire.'

'Sir, you should get some rest.'

His breathing has begun to drag, like a coiled snake rasping out of tangled roots. Deller's face in candlelight is ashen, save for unhealthy veins on his cheeks, red mycelia, like a consumptive's blush. His eyes roam restlessly in the void. 'Did I betray my gift? Ought I to have gone to Italy . . . to become a painter of first rank . . . instead of seeking out the war in England?'

'Mr Deller . . .'

'Arrogant *knave*.'

'We could perhaps resume tomorrow?'

'I thought I could contribute. To the improvement. Of man's estate.'

'At least take a little food . . .'

'Now *my* estate decays. I have lost my servants and neglected my daughter's welfare . . . *William*.' He throws out his arms and William kneels at his feet to take them. The old man's face is savage with remorse. 'When the Lord Protector died . . . God forgive me . . . I sailed to Holland. It was to visit my old tutor, whose health was failing . . . But I had another, less noble purpose. I introduced myself to courtiers in exile . . . as the man who tried to rescue the dead King's art collection . . . Thus a true but impotent grievance . . . was dressed up as political loyalty. All to secure patronage . . . in case King Charles was restored.'

William feels, with scant comprehension, the agitation in Deller's body. Where is the shame in what he did?

'Look in the chest, Thomas. For God's sake . . . You will find another pouch, a leather pouch. *Go*.'

William obeys the old man's orders. What did he just call him? He takes a candle to the chest and searches inside. Is he looking for a sketch of Belinda? Some document that will make his task achievable?

Returning with the leather pouch to Mr Deller's side, he extracts four worn and faded sheets of paper. Roundheads are drinking water from their upturned helmets; their faces stained from battle, or from marching on a muddy track. A copse of oaks seems to swelter on a purple plain. 'Do you see them? Do you see?' Another picture shows a thief hanged from a gallows, a loaf of bread (doubtless his crime) exposed beside him.

'Sir – what am I looking for?'

'The young man in the hat. Do you have him?'

On the most damaged sheet of all, where ancient folds have made a blank cross in the painting, William discerns the figure of a young man in a broad straw hat, sitting under a starveling oak and reading a book.

'There is an inscription.'

'*Nosce ipsum.*'

'Know thyself . . . I ought to have given it to him. But I was afraid to have him in my house.' Mr Deller reddens as he clears his throat of some obstruction. Half choking, he pronounces judgement on himself. 'I am weighed in the balance and am found wanting.'

'Shall I call your daughter?'

Mr Deller is confused and rambling. William tries to quell his anxiety; but the old man is racked by a desiccated cough. His mouth is distorted by the force of it; his throat strains, its veins distended. He fumbles about the table in front of him. William tries to anticipate Mr Deller's needs and steers the glass into his way. Contact fails and the plate of untouched sugar cakes falls to the floor.

'Look at her, William . . . Save her for me.'

Too late, William tries to steady the candle. The flame is extinguished in its fall; but Deller does not know this, or how close to him his protector stands.

'Help! Help!'

Perhaps he means to catch the candle, or smother the presumed flames. William sees the old man lurching forward. There is a nauseating *crack* as the side of his head strikes the table.

William finds himself running to the door. He shouts into the darkness. 'Miss Deller! *Cynthia!*'

Doors slam in the household; stairs rumble. William is bending over the prone figure when Cynthia appears, swiftly followed by the maid. William sees the horror in their faces. 'He fell,' he says apologetically.

'Father . . .'

Mr Deller stirs and groans, his hand rising to his temple. 'I dropped the candle.'

'It went out, Father.'

'I thought I would burn.'

'There is no flame.'

William, standing back to allow the women their authority, feels himself to blame. 'Are you hurt, sir?'

'I . . . Take me to bed. Let me breathe a while.'

Collectively they lift him, William upsetting the table with his heel.

Mr Deller has paid for his luxuries. His mouth is carious: William tastes his rotten breath as they carry him to his chamber. Can Cynthia be the strongest among them? She shows no emotion as she tends to her father's comfort.

Carefully they ease him on to the bed. He coughs horribly. 'Let me . . . let me catch my breath. I am . . . a doltish . . . old man.'

From a trestle table in an obscure corner, the maid produces a bowl of water. Cynthia, seated on the bed, wrings out a flannel. 'Do not be startled, Father. I am going to wet your brow.' She flannels him. William, standing awkwardly aside as though intruding on a scene of intimacy, looks for evidence of a wound on Deller's temple. A little blood wells up from a deep purple bruise.

'Oh,' Mr Deller moans. The water and his daughter's presence seem to soothe him a little. There is no mistaking, thinks William, the true cause of his agitation. It is the portrait he must finish.

'Mr Stroud,' says the old man, 'you should sleep.'

'Shh now, Father. I will prepare the guest room.'

Cynthia dips the flannel and passes it across Deller's brow. William watches the flexion of her fingers. They do not belong to a leisured gentlewoman, with their prominent veins and scurfed knuckles. Her fingernails are chewed nacre.

'Look again, Mr Stroud.' Water fills the dry channels of Deller's face. 'Look again at the painting. In the light of day.'

'I will.'

'And . . . soon . . . ?'

'You shall have an answer.'

Cynthia leans over her father, shielding him from William's gaze. 'Quiet, Father. Rest now, please.'

The old man's breathing grows heavy and uniform as Cynthia and William withdraw from his chamber. He is already asleep when the latch comes to rest.

1660

Frederick has appeared in the hallway wearing a long shirt and hose, his pellucid eyes seeping from interrupted sleep. Digby follows the old man up the stairs. He would address him in brotherly terms but the cud from his dispute with Deller sours his tongue. He looks down at the servant's withered shanks, at the hole in the stockings from which pasty skin shows, and longs to be alone, to consider what has passed and make sense of that intemperate exchange. They pass a number of closed doors on the landing. Digby makes out the sterterous breathing of Bathsheba and imagines a voluminous matron with breasts like butterballs rising and falling. He wonders which of the doors conceals Belinda Deller.

'It is a new Flood,' says Frederick in a whisper, without turning his head, so that Digby is uncertain whether it was meant for him. Here, in the very heart of the manor, he can no longer hear the rush of rain: only their footfalls and the odd complaint of ancient timbers. The maid's snores diminish. They have come to the guest bedroom. Frederick holds open the door with his shoulder. 'No belongings, sir?' Digby shakes his head and explores the room with his eyes. The servant's lantern drifts away. Shadows lengthen and merge. Then Frederick returns.

'Shall I wake you, sir? The master breaks fast at . . .'

'No, thank you, friend. I rise with the sun.' Digby just has time to read contempt on the servant's face before he bows – spurning familiarity – and withdraws.

Standing alone in partial shadow, Digby sighs and yawns. To hold off his darker thoughts, he makes a slow inspection of the chamber: stroking with finger and thumb the damask and tapestries and embroidered bed hangings. He wonders whether Belinda Deller made these, and applies the flat of his hand to the material, imagining her quick fingers at work, her head bowed and her lips pursed in creative absorption.

He extinguishes the image in the cold washbasin. He must be master of his thoughts. It is night and he has drunk; the Devil will be near. Looking up from the water, he is startled by his reflection in the mirror of the dressing table. He watches it for a while, until with a familiar and frightening lurch it ceases to make sense to him. He ignores the toothpowder in its bowl (knowing what it most likely contains) and rubs his teeth with salt from his pewter travel box. From the same he extracts a scraper and diligently picks the scurf from his gums. When he has finished, he stares vacuously at the spittle from his rinsing.

Deller hates him.

Irritably he undresses, his clothes exhaling a hon-eyed fetor as he throws them to the floor. Bending to remove his breeches, he suffers a painful spasm in his bowels. He looks in panic for a chamber pot, sees the door of the closet ajar and lowers himself on the close-stool.

Digby watches his pale knees trembling. He curses himself for his failure with Deller; he curses Deller for abandoning, with such pretence of philosophy, the eternal truths they once espoused. The spasm in his guts eases as the miasma rises, and Digby realises that his jaw is locked. Making a mental effort to unclench it, he moans at the sudden release of pain. How everything is corrupted by his despair. Why must he suffer, why alone uphold the memory of defeat, when his fellows prosper in their moral degradation? Trees breathe in the fields, boys play in the streams, but Digby feels trapped in a bell of cold glass. He cannot enjoy the spring for its buds contain the fruits of decay. Injustice, cruelty, the prosperity of sinners: all persuade him that Time is near its end. The world is the womb of death.

Having wiped himself and rinsed his fingers, Digby undresses completely. On the coverlet of the bed he discovers a parcel of dried flowers. He lifts it to his nose. It is the same fragrance he encountered in the hall, though fading now along with the colours. Digby tastes her name in his mouth. *Belinda*. He drops the parcel of flowers on the trestle table, parts the clean sheets and clambers into bed. Immediately, his back hurts. It is a sharp reminder. Digby crawls on all fours to the foot of the bed, wraps his still-damp shirt about his waist, for modesty's sake, and sinks to his knees on the polished boards. He recites the Lord's Prayer and, to ease his troubled spirits, the twenty-third psalm. Even as he speaks the words, his thoughts are elsewhere.

One day soon he will be found out. Spurned by politic authority, he has been operating as an apothecary without a licence. *For Thine is the Kingdom, for ever and ever. Amen.* Why did he not speak of these troubles to his host? Nathaniel thinks his motives are godly when they are not, or not entirely. The Lord leads Thomas Digby beside still waters, yet he dwells in the parched desert of his debts. A table is prepared in the presence of his enemies and Digby imagines them clearly: his creditors and errand boys, waiting for him in some pisspot alley, staves and fists at the ready. *Thou hast anointed my head with oil; my cup runneth over.* In Massachusetts, he has heard, there is no imprisonment for debt. Might that be the freedom of which he speaks? *Surely goodness and mercy shall follow me all the days of my life: and I will dwell in the house of the Lord for ever.*

The psalm recited, Digby returns to bed – and to the pain in his lumbar. The mattress is smooth and yielding; instead of straw, his pillow contains eiderdown. Digby sighs several times, then rises on one elbow to blow out the candle. *Snuffed from all corruption shalt thou be.* He lies back, allowing darkness to close over him. The moon, hidden by storm clouds, gives no light. He feels his eyes adapting to the dark; he shuts them to bid sleep come.

At Dover today, looking for future passage, he suffered mockery and suspicion. For the New World, men said, he needed to go to *Bristol*. Merchant seamen laughed at his ignorance; then asked why he should want to leave England. Digby escaped to the streets and glimpsed the King, his enemy.

What would it cost to take passage to America? He has used up all his savings to buy the horse. He has no experience of ships and would need to boast of his surgical skills. Toby at least could offer carpentry but what of the others when he finds them? Thinking of wives and daughters in tow, he imagines a mariner leering and turns brusquely on to his side.

He leaves the salt air of Dover, with its cheering crowds and grim-faced soldiers, its flotsam of bewildered foreign sailors. He rides his horse on the downs. The chalk meadows are a blur beneath him. Flocks of sheep bleat and scatter. Carrion some-where is attracting kites. He sees the circling birds and thinks: It is a dream of England that has died . . .

Now, in this fragrant bed, Digby is bone weary. His body remembers every jolt of the journey. His heels are dreaming of stirrups and seem to kick of their own accord. The darkness swirls about him. As when, in childhood, he embarked on a fever, he feels the bed churning. The chamber closes in on him. Then the walls and ceiling lurch back, and he shrinks on the stark plain of the mattress, hearing again Nathaniel's angry words, his refusal to join the enterprise.

The painter's face is lost in shadow. The flames behind him are the fires of Hell.

Somewhere in the manor's labyrinth, a door or window bangs shut. Is it Deller going to bed? The noise is followed by a percussion from diverse places. Digby feels a momentary chill; he shivers as though a ghost has entered his chamber. A great gust of wind shakes the trees outside. Breakers of rain lash against the roof. The house creaks like a galleon at sea . . . Then quietness . . . The rain ceases, the wind seems to have blown itself out, and Digby fancies he can hear the trees shedding the corpse of the storm. How gladly he would partake of their respite; but his spirits will not settle. What was it the old servant whispered? A second Flood is coming. Why, so it must be. Was not the executed Charles one of the kings of Revelation, who gave his powers to the Beast? The violent opposition that Digby encounters daily must prove that the end is approaching. He pictures the grimaces of men in the cockpit in Shoe Lane. Sometimes he goes there, in humble imitation of Our Lord among sinners, to speak of the other world that is possible. With Toby and Robert, his companions, he attends the prizefights at the Bear Garden, averting his gaze from the bloodied faces and raw knuckles, breathing through his mouth to endure the sweat and tobacco smells. They search for the spectator who shuts his eyes in moral shame, or winces in sympathy when a fighter falls. *This* one, *that* one, may yet be saved. Then Digby and his companions speak of the common, of the Grace that fell like sunlight on a hill in Surrey long ago, and how men might clear the way for King Jesus. Why not join us, brother, in our flight to the New World?

Tickled by pillow feathers, Digby coughs; a mizzle of spit settles on his nose. Of course, the voyage will not be without its terrors. Clinging to the rigging in a gale, with their guts heaving and the spray like a watery lash across their faces, they will long for England's solid earth. Compared with the gluttonous deep, the very stocks of Lambeth might seem a paradise. They will need men of eloquence to keep their spirits afloat – a new Winstanley, or William

Dell. *He that fears God is free from all other fears.* Surely they will not drown if Providence is with them?

Stretching out under the sheets, Digby presses his face into the warmth of his bare bicep. He must sleep; he is in need of sleep's medicine. But he has not considered his host, the argument with his host, or what he might do to sway him. Is there still hope for that? The true Nathaniel is entombed in that portly flesh. What formula can Digby find to disinter him?

He turns his head and drags his body after. He ceases, for a moment, to listen to his thoughts and hears, in that hiatus, very faintly, a repetitive droning, like the sound of a heavy chest being steadily pushed across a floor. With eyes shut and ears tingling, Digby tries to make sense of it. Of course: those are Bathsheba's snores resonating through the boards. He considers them a kind of insult, the smug display of another's easy commerce with sleep. Enviously he listens; and begins to doubt his theory. The sound is too deep for a woman. Though unable to locate it, he decides that it must belong to Nathaniel, sleeping apart from his wife in order not to trouble her pregnant rest.

Digby remembers a night on the common: the air flavoured with gorse, the cool sand between his fingers, and the distant churring of nightjars. The moon was fat as they lay about the feathers of a dead fire (it was so warm they had no need of one) and wallowed in their liberty, young rogues all and equals under God. Digby, who had started speaking, looked up from his pillow of heather to find that he was addressing the stars; for his companions had fallen asleep. Nat Deller was there, and resting her tousled head on his shoulder . . . what was the girl's name? That must have been their last night together.

Digby meditates on Time's symmetry. Now as then, he listens to Nathaniel sleeping. The house, the soggy downs and all the country must be replete with dreams, which yet take up less space in the world than a mote of dust.

Aches and longings in Digby's body dwindle. It occurs to him that he has never known, for certain, the hopes and beliefs of his former companion. Their friendship, all those years ago, was easy and instinctual. Each was comfortable with the other and they enjoyed talking. Was it that they both meant to change their surroundings: Digby in social terms and Nathaniel—? *His* chief purpose in Cobham had been to sketch and paint. He used to seek out the flimsy shade of a birch thicket and there, his tools laid out beside him in the grass, he would scan the distant purple hills, shimmering with heat, until inspiration, as he called it, set his fingers roving. Digby, along with the children whom Nathaniel could not refuse, was one of the few permitted to watch the pictures emerging: that amorphous shape becoming a cow, those tangles of wire transformed, by a smudging thumb, into an impression of wind-threshed foliage. Nat Deller pursued his craft: *so*. But he worked at furze cutting with the rest of them, though he was slow and unfit, prone to great sweats and flushing cheeks, and would soon declare his compulsion to set this scene or that sky to paper. In his difference he was indulged by some, resented by others. A few made no secret of their enmity towards him. Did Digby defend his friend, in those muttering circles, out of misplaced affection? Was it possible they were right, those who considered the painter an impostor? Wiser voices argued otherwise. All men of faith were needed, they said, for the success of their enterprise. Warned of his position, Nathaniel had helped with the livestock, flapping his cap to steer the cattle and gripping (inexpertly, like apothecary Digby) the scrabbling ewe caught up in a thicket. Many times, in private conversation, he expressed his admiration for their community. He enjoyed – that was his word – *enjoyed* the simplicity of their life, though scores of weathered faces, mangled by toil, ought to have scotched the word in his throat.

They were scything the tall grass by the river when it happened. The whole illumination lasted only an instant, the time of a yaffle's flight through a glade, yet it was long enough for Digby. He saw Nathaniel rest on his scythe handle and gaze into the distance. His eyes turned glassy with dreaming, and Digby perceived how far removed his rich friend was from the unlettered peasants who daily flocked to the heath. He did not belong in such company. If the enterprise failed, he would still be able to prosper. There was another life for him to resume . . . Yes, the present Digby reasons, or allows reason to flow through his numbness, it was his security, more than any turn of phrase or detail of dress, which set the painter apart. He was there by choice instead of desperate need. For most who came, the common offered a last hope. To Deller it must have seemed a kind of game.

Digby perceives all this without emotion. He is slipping, without knowing it, into the easeful mist. His limbs are at rest. The bed has stilled beneath him, sparing him just enough mind to wonder whether death might not be like this: enabling one to see the world clearly without suffering the stings of outrage or regret. People will always be opaque to him, as often to themselves. Only God has God's eye. It is emerging from the clouds now. The chamber fills with its lunar glow. But Digby does not know it. For a few hours, he is free.

1680

They stand for a minute, maybe more, like parents outside a sick child's bedchamber, hoping to hear nothing: no cough, no sigh or whimper of distress. William sooner than Cynthia allows his attention to wander. He looks at her. Her mouth is open, her lips a little moist. Her eyes, subordinate to another sense, float in imitation of her sightless father; but she cannot resist his gaze for long. Their eye-beams tangle. Bashfully they disengage and William reverences, in mock and earnest gallantry, extending an arm towards the staircase with a meaning that eludes them both.

'Have you,' says Cynthia, studying William's shirt, 'had enough to eat?'

William does not wish to appear greedy; yet he sees an opportunity to prolong their encounter. 'Your sugar cakes were very good.'

'Did you dine before you came?'

'No.'

'Then jumbals cannot make up for a missed supper. Will you have a little broth?'

'If there is some.'

'On the stove. Lizzie's recipe, if you do not mind—'

'That would please me.'

'—leeks.' They fail to suppress their smiles. 'To the kitchen. We will take the servants' way.'

As she leads William along the corridor to the winding stairs, Cynthia worries what significance a gentleman might attach to her invitation. The kitchen is a woman's domain, her place of labour and her sanctum. Did she leave it tidy enough?

'So this is how you came so quickly,' William says, placing his feet carefully on the narrow steps. Cynthia precedes him, her taper's flame yearning towards her bosom. Steadying himself with his elbow on the walls, he takes the opportunity to watch her unhindered. He sees a thin parting of pale skin and gossamer down of pleached hairs on her nape. Has any man, he wonders, kissed her there? The narrowness of the stairwell concentrates her fragrance: a sort of rosewater mixed with flour and something poignantly unplaceable, the redolence of her skin and hair.

'Be careful of the last step, Mr Stroud. It is uneven.'

To think that she might be his! Mr Deller could not have been more explicit. William has only to paint a dead woman's face as best he can. No one will know whether he has failed or succeeded; and it would be a kindness to ease an old man's passing.

In the kitchen Cynthia goes to the stove. She carries

a black pot to the fire and, shedding her gloves, leaves the broth to simmer. William watches her ordinary movements. He likes very much her plainness: the absence of face-paint and patches that one might expect on a lady. Nor is she ruddy, swollen by sun and wind like so many Kent lasses. Aside from a few childhood scars (including one, above her left eye, which he finds almost alluring), she has unblemished skin. He observes what seems to be her placid concentration as she lays out for him, like a good wife, a bowl and wooden spoon. He smiles with benevolence at the constellation of freckles on her throat, though he knows these are ill regarded and can never be openly praised. A fig for the world's opinions! William congratulates himself on the independence of his tastes, for Cynthia is not fashionably black but ginger blonde.

'Will you have some water, Mr Stroud? It comes from the spring.'

'Thank you.' Cynthia must not sense his arousal. William looks about himself for distraction and notices that the kitchen is filled with flower pots: on the table, on shelves where jars and almanacs stand, on every window sill. He stoops to appreciate an aromatic sprig. 'Charming,' he says.

'Necessary for the flies.' Cynthia sees, an instant before William does, his coat draped about the struts of a chair and then his hat beside the chopping board.

'I brought them here,' she explains hastily, 'because of the warmth.'

Indeed, the kitchen is the only place where a fire still burns. William nods and smiles when she invites him to sit. They have much to say that cannot easily be spoken.

'Do you think,' William ventures, 'that your father will sleep the night?'

'Pray God, for his sake.'

Cynthia returns to the stove and lifts the lid on the broth, releasing a genie of steam. William's mouth waters at the smell of leeks and potatoes. She lifts the pot skilfully, making light of its probable weight and, armed with a formidable ladle, begins to serve William his supper. He looks at her hands. They are pink and swollen, more like his mother's than those of a lady. She gives him, with apologies, a crust of bread. William thanks her again and, taking the utmost care not to spill any of it, lifts the spoon with the broth to his lips. At home they slurp such fare noisily. His father, if the food is hot, will chew it open mouthed like a dog eating marrow. William must endeavour to show more decorum. He senses her melancholy eyes on his movements. 'It must be hard work,' he says between mouthfuls, 'keeping so big a house in order.'

Cynthia concurs with her eyes. She must tell him nothing – and yet no, she would tell him *all* – about her labours. For want of servants (the women who come from the farms are garrulous and take too obvious a pleasure in her discomfort) it is *she* who must scour the kitchen floor with sand; she who helps sweep the rooms and makes polish for the furniture. With Lizzie's help, she buys food for the larder and stokes the fires. Some days Mr Deller must make do with cold meat, for there is no time to cook. 'I have,' she says, 'more work to do than I might wish for. Our washing used to be done by whitsters from the village.' She trails off and William eats his broth of disappointment. Are they, then, so impoverished? 'Jem grows much of our food in the garden. And we have a boy, Lizzie's nephew, who fetches bread and such.'

'Is he the lad who brought me your letter?'

Cynthia nods. 'Soon he will be apprenticed to the blacksmith and we shall lose him.'

William frowns in sympathy. She watches him from the corner of her eye: how he leans over his bowl, sinking the spoon until it fills with broth (pondweed, she called it when she was a child), then leans back, loath to display rustic manners, and allows the filaments of leek to drip dry before he lifts the spoon to his mouth. He catches a rogue drop with his thumb and she pretends to ignore it, plucking dead seed pods from the dry melilot on the table. If her father bruised himself in his fall, she must make a poultice from it tomorrow.

'Is it good, Mr Stroud?'

'Excellent. Thank you.'

What did the two men talk about? What have they planned for her? She watches William tearing his bread, the sinews flexing in his hands. He is not handsome, exactly, with his large, somewhat flattened nose and those narrow, unjustly parsimonious lips. But his hands, which are big like her father's (though lacking an old man's paw-like swelling), have a kind of animal innocence that reflects well on their owner. William has gathered up his sleeves, exposing his tanned wrists and the arterial veins, like muscles, on their paler undersides. The dark hairs that grow aslant his knuckles ought to be unsightly; yet it pleases her to look at them. Comparing what she can discern of him with her father's hollow frame and the scrawny, faintly amphibian body of their gardener, she realises: William Stroud is the finest man she knows.

'May I ask you a question, Miss Deller?'

'Please.'

William begins to wipe his bowl with the soft of his bread; he catches himself in the act and relents. 'Your father seems to have been disappointed in his profession. Would that be fair to say? I mean that neither the Commonwealth nor the court valued his talent. He was ill rewarded for his truest work and lacked patronage to pursue his ideals.'

Cynthia offers no response.

'Was he hoping for preferment from the King? Until Peter Lely became Principal Painter in his place, so to speak?'

'My father has never confided in me on professional matters.'

William, feeling somewhat scolded, accepts her reply in silence. Cynthia does not wish to be forbidding. She ought to meet him in conversation instead of killing his every question; for only when he speaks has she licence to look at him. She remembers their first encounter. William then was a gangling, nervous youth, with nascent down on his upper lip and a voice that wavered between bass racket and shrill fife. In all her twelve years she had known nothing like it. Her first instinct was envy: to see a miller's son promoted by her father to the semblance of a country squire, entrusted with books that she was forbidden to read and learning, as she was never permitted to try, to paint in her father's shadow. She used to call on them, having unburdened the maid, bearing cakes and small beer, just to see the dark boy at his lessons; to be, however briefly, in the company of those very different men, mature and immature, familiar and unknown. Whenever William frowned, his cheeks blushing and his gaze resolutely fixed on his papers (did she disgust him, for him to look away?), she would be reminded of the apprentice painters whom she had seen, years earlier, sweating in the summer heat of the city, applying background touches to her father's paintings.

'He was prolific,' says William, 'for one who worked alone.'

'Not quite alone, Mr Stroud.'

'Oh, but . . . did he not? I understood that he worked alone.'

'So he did, when he was here.'

'He had assistants, then, in London?'

Cynthia plucks at her thumb and, under the heat of William's enquiry, looks down at her dress front. 'Perhaps my memory is false – or I am mistaken. Either way, it hardly matters now.' Fool. She is cooling him with her distant manner. William collects breadcrumbs from the table with his forefinger, a frown like a scar forming above the bridge of his nose. '*Oh*.' Rising abruptly, Cynthia gropes along one of the higher shelves. 'He said I am to give you this.'

William receives from her hands a small case made of walnut and newly burnished with linseed oil. He recognises Mr Deller's watercolour box. 'Good Lord!' He flicks at the latch in hope but finds, where blocks of paint used to be, merely stains in ivory. His thumb, of its own accord, rubs against the bone of an empty socket. What is the meaning of this? He feels blood rise to his face and is powerless to stanch it.

The old man must be mocking him. From the desert of his talent, William is no more capable of making art than Deller would have been with an empty paintbox.

'He had it in his youth,' says Cynthia. 'It is a valuable object. You should restore it to its purpose.'

William nods. He smiles and feels a bitter muscle twitch in his jaw.

'You remember,' says Cynthia, 'what Henry Peacham wrote in *The Complete Gentleman* . . .'

'You have read that?'

' "No man is accomplished who cannot work in miniature." '

William is confounded by this proof of her learning. He recalls that dispiriting book, how far reading it made him feel from his goal – a flea at the foothills. As a young man he wrote little and without style; he pounded through country dances so gracefully mimicked in grander circles. Only art seemed to offer some hope of improvement, and he applied himself assiduously to his studies, copying the standards of gesture and anatomy. (The eye, Peacham wrote, requires great conceit in the making. It gives a taste of the spirit and disposition of the mind. This being so, what could William know of Nathaniel Deller?)

'You seem displeased,' says Cynthia.

'I am not. It makes me more indebted to your father.'

'I believe I win on that count, Mr Stroud.'

William shuts the watercolour box with his suspicions inside it, and tries to brighten. 'Oh, granted,' he says.

Cynthia feels momentary resentment. Why should this young man, almost a stranger, receive this hallowed gift? And what *is* the debt she owes her father? Life? A thing she never asked for. Then she remembers her Christian duty. She must honour her father; and to counter her ingratitude she reminds herself that he is dying. The epicure is interred already in his flesh; the stoic also. He whimpered when last she applied cantharides to his skin. As for cupping, her father used to insist on it for purging his melancholy bile. It is proof of mortal sickness that he can no longer withstand such rough physic. The sherry that she served tonight was a concession to his ailing pride. Ordinarily she gives him milch-asses' milk for his delicate stomach, as though he were changed back to a child.

'Your father was always generous,' says William. 'He gave me prints of Rubens: *Susanna and the Elders*, *The Descent from the Cross*. And, when his sight began to fail, his sketching desk.'

Cynthia wanly smiles. Things that fall into uselessness: objects that die without use. They are hateful to him.

'Tell me about your father's blindness.' William

sees her flinch and yet he persists. 'He sent me away before the worst of it. I was banished from your company.'

Something catches in Cynthia's throat. She must cough to clear it.

'I mean, Miss Deller . . . What was it like, for him and for you, when he slipped into darkness?'

That word again. How she has lived in the shadow of his shadows. Her father's clumsy fingers, snuffling like moles in the bewildering air; his weeping before her when he could no longer determine the colour of her dress: all these sorrows she has carried in silence, without daring to complain. She fixes her gaze on William's hands where they rest, palms down, on the table.

'He went to London,' she says. 'He went to have an operation. To remove the clouded apple of his eye.' Couching, they called it. She finds intolerable the thought of her father's pain: tied by silken ropes to a chair, struggling to see and yet not to see the descending implements.

'I had no idea. When was this?'

'Four years ago. I went with him. *That* was my second visit to London.'

'And there was no improvement?'

The physician seemed revolted to be explaining himself to a *girl*. He couched the truth in mellifluous euphemism; but from his pallor and sweat she gleaned more meaning. He had botched the procedure. The occlusions remained. 'What you have witnessed tonight, Mr Stroud . . . For his sake and for mine, remember my father as he was, not as he has become.'

'He is still a noble man.'

'Do you know the story of Tobit?'

William scours his shreds of Scripture. 'The man blinded by a sparrow's doings?'

'Just so.' A hot load of guano in the eyes. A very foolish tale, no doubt. She sees William smirk but disdains to mirror him. 'My father wanted to paint the story before it became prophetic for him. You remember how it goes. Old Tobit is in despair. It is cold winter in exile. He is blind and infirm. His son comes to save him . . .'

'The miraculous fish!'

'He applies its gall to Tobit's eyes. The old man is healed. At the instant of his restoration, he sees that his son's companion is the Archangel Raphael. There is a blast of heavenly light, and the visitor is gone.'

William nods at her story, but wonders what she means by it.

'The radiance that Tobit saw was divine, Mr Stroud. It was God's light and he was permitted to see it because his earthly sight had failed.'

'Do you mean . . . ?'

'My father has not been so consoled. I see no sign

in him of inward eyes.' Cynthia rises, making a brisk gesture for William not to follow, and clears the table of his spoon and bowl. 'Has he spoken to you about *ingenium*?'

'*Ingenium*?'

'The divine spirit of creation.'

'I think so.'

'For him it takes a particular form.'

William feels icy dew pricking at his nape. 'Yes?'

'A woman in white, his divine inspiration, appearing in visions and dreams. Always she comes to presage a new work. Without her, nothing would happen on the canvas.'

'His muse, then?'

'He has told me of this only lately, Mr Stroud. I do not properly understand it.'

'Does she have a name?'

'A *name*?'

'Is it . . . ? What do you think she signifies?'

Cynthia shrugs. 'Creative impulse. Spiritual need. My father's ghostly longing has only deepened in his affliction. Before, he could make some use of it. It cannot now take form in the visible world.'

Returning to her seat, she sees William looking haggard and pale. He chews his lower lip and avoids her gaze. Why should he think, at this moment, of his own father? Abraham Stroud is not burnished by sun: he is ruddy with troubles.

He lives in dread of a bad harvest, of angry customers refusing his prices, of fire sparking off the runner stone and burning down the mill. William hates his father's silences and the soil whence they grow. Abraham laughs with a stoop of apology, as another man clears his throat. He speaks of a beautiful day in the accents of rain.

'My father,' says William, 'I used to consider a cruel and heartless man. Miss Deller, he has been spared your father's misfortune. And yet it concerns me that he be considered justly.'

She watches, wanting to touch him, and listens.

'He is not without finer qualities. I think he *would* be kind had not life taught him to conceal his goodness. Sometimes, as a boy, I suffered blows because he wished not to strike me. I forced him to act *against* his nature, you see. And by dint of this compulsion, his nature altered to the thing he would not have it be.' William's voice sounds to his ears dispassionate, as he intends. But there is a strange weight to Cynthia's gaze. Her sympathy pains him and arouses him. The arousal is not priapic; it boils in the pit of his stomach, a raw, unappeasable burning that compels him to look down into the grate, giving him the very semblance of sorrow that he would avoid.

'Is this a mature understanding of your father? Did you hold these notions when you were a boy, when he gave you those bruises which you wore to your lessons?'

She noticed those, then? Her father never said a word. 'I think,' says William, 'I had not the words to express them until this night.'

Sea coals in the grate ruffle and expire. Cynthia seems to fill the shadows. William looks down at his hands in the violent apprehension that hers are drawing near.

They are not.

He is conscious suddenly of a deep lassitude. He feels nauseous and dizzy. Is it sleep which makes him seem to drift towards her? Her eyes are dark pools for him to drown in, which she guards from his approach. 'Cynthia,' he says. 'Why will you not call me by my familiar name?'

She has no answer. She looks at his sloping, mournful expression. There is a harsh cry outside, followed by gibbering noises. She looks in relief at the window, which is slightly ajar, causing violets to tremble on the sill. They hear a whimper, sharply curtailed; then silence, save for the breeze and the slumber of the manor house. 'One of the owls,' Cynthia says, 'has caught her supper.'

'A vole, do you suppose?'

'I hope a rat.' She has evaded his question. Now she hears herself blathering, like a fishwife at market, about her battles with vermin: how they pilfer from the larder and gnaw at the heels of chairs, how they have begun to shred the tapestries in the hall.

William fights the drooping of his eyelids. He does not want to leave yet. He tells her, in a thick voice like a drinker, about the mice in his father's mill. Finding them in the corn bins, he used to urge his sisters to cast them down the hopper. Then he would try to catch them on the stone floor, pounding with a stick the flipping brown bodies. It seemed a great lark; until one day he stamped on a mouse and felt the hot pulp through his shoe. Then disgust and shame put an end to his play.

'Mr Stroud, you should sleep.'

'What time is it?'

'Late. Or early.' And, because of the nervous flicker in his eyes, she adds: 'You cannot ride back now. You would fall snoring from your saddle.'

William laughs. 'I dare say I would.'

She offers to lead him to his room. He thanks her for the meal and, more importantly, for her company. She holds her hands folded behind her back: it would be useless to reach for them in a mock-gallant kiss.

They take the winding staircase back to the upper floor, William cupping his hand about his candle, Cynthia bearing a lantern.

The chamber to which she leads him lies two rooms east of Mr Deller's. He listens for sounds of breathing and thinks he discerns them, very faint and feeble, though it may be the maid.

Cynthia hesitates in the doorway and William enters alone. He sees an old bed, four-postered, with hangings in faded yellow and peach. Bare plaster retains the phantom outlines of tapestries. There is a close odour of mould and moth dust.

'Lizzie put spring water in the basin. And the sheets are clean.'

'Thank you.' He watches her reflection in the bed-stand's mottled mirror. Her image shows more faint and tired. 'You must sleep too.'

'I intend to, Mr Stroud.'

He wants to rest his aching bones on the bed. She does not withdraw from the entrance; instead, she casts a glance down the corridor and then steps decisively into the chamber, pulling the door within an inch of closure.

'Did you see her portrait, Mr Stroud?' William's sleepy bonhomie fades. She *knows*, then? All that foolish secrecy for nothing. He opens his lips and Cynthia grows impatient. 'What did he show you? I must be told.'

Her face looks strange; there is a force throbbing in her eyes. 'Paintings,' says William. 'Of yourself, reading. And resting. And then others, from a more distant past.'

'You must find them too dark.' William equivocally purses his lips. He tastes a flippant reply in his mouth and wisely swallows it. Cynthia is in earnest. 'My youth was spent in darkness like tonight. When his sight began to fail, my father withdrew from the world. He painted no more landscapes, would see no one. You were not banished from him, Mr Stroud. He banished himself. From humanity. And I went with him. The curtains, even on bright days, were always drawn. The windows were shut. When he would attempt to work, he made private portraits, using only candlelight and lanterns. His household, his estate, discandied like tallow.'

'The portrait of your mother is no dark interior.'

'I have never seen it.' William sees the agitation in her chest. She lets the lantern hang at her knees, so that her face in shadow is unreadable. 'Well? You must be my eyes, Mr Stroud. What of this painting? What of my mother?'

'She . . . occupies the centre of the canvas . . . in a garden of great beauty. She sits, with child, in a summer garden.'

'What does she look like?'

'He could not complete it.'

'And that is why he summoned you here tonight?'

They stand silent in each other's gaze. Then Cynthia curtsies, her dress sighing on the floorboards. William reverences like an alderman. She is departing: he must crampon himself to a poster for restraint.

She opens the door and stops, half gone. She raises the lantern a few inches, to waist height, sufficiently to see her guest and be discerned by him.

'I am,' she says, 'his only mutable creation.'

1650

She fancied the mountain was breathing. It was strange the way it came at you, like a ghost in the darkness. He told her it was the heat of the sun trapped all day in the earth. And now set free by the moon.

Besides, he said, this is no mountain.

She put her hand in his. Walking uphill through a tunnel of bracken, scratching their ears on gorse and feeling the tug of brambles at their shins, they basked in the heat given off by the hill. Yet a faint unease continued to trouble him. The girl at his side, so bright and vital, was life itself and he was a bloodless tick attracted to her warmth. Perhaps she sensed his self-reproach, for in the shelter of a birch thicket she kissed his chin and rubbed her nose against his neck. He would be jolly for her in spite of his forebodings.

What monstrous bread did she think was being baked in this oven?

She frowned, pursuing his metaphor. She caught it. 'Not monstrous. It is our future. Enough for everyone.'

He looked at her in the dappled moonlight. Was it ignorance or inherited wisdom which gave her hope? It was a mystery to him what world she had come from. Could she even read? 'Let us contemplate your future,' he said.

They crept to the edge of the copse, where the hill gave way to tangled thorns and brambles and dissolving sandbank. There used to be a badger sett in that cheerless spot, until the Diggers filled in its holes and killed the beasts for their bristles. That was early in the colony's history, after the exodus from St George's Hill, and they had needed goods to barter for food. Nathaniel had been saddened by the sett's destruction but glad to partake of the browsells and frangible oast cakes that followed.

From this vantage point they could see most of the common, even as far as the glistening river. (Mole, it was called. Burrowing through English soil.) He noted carefully the silvery seam of grassland dotted with browsing cattle, and the black deposits of gorse whose flowers were faded. The heather, where it had not been burned or gathered for kindling, was dark grey like powdered charcoal, its constellations of pink flowers extinguished. Occasionally a dog's bark, or adult voices, flew up to them, like birds from bracken. He looked for the settlements on the heath, his eyes threading the smoke that drifted from cooking fires. The dozens of huts made of wood and topped with furze (he shivered to think how readily they would burn) scarcely intruded on the landscape but seemed, rather, excrescences from it, as though the commoners themselves were moulded of earth and birch and heather. Susannah clumsily caressed his ankle with her foot. The skin of her toes was hard and calloused; he moved to dissuade her, not yet willing to relinquish the scene. There survived a thin sliver of light to the west – a gash, like a revelation of gold in velvet of the deepest blue.

'Look,' he said, wanting to charge her vision. 'It is as if God has ripped a tear in the fabric of night. And that is the light behind everything: the *coelum empyreum*, or effulgence of heaven.'

Susannah began to run her palm along his thigh. The world constricted for him and he permitted himself to kiss her. She was very small and compact and he was obliged to bow to reach her mouth. With the hungry tug of her lips and her timidly darting tongue, she was quite unlike the passionless drabs he had known in Amsterdam. Then, for all the urgency of his desire, their bodies had been distasteful to him. But now, with this child of the heath, her very spit was intoxicating. He heard her small, plaintive moans as he burrowed with his fingers beneath her skirt. He longed to nuzzle her, and half knelt to kiss the top of her breasts. Only when his fingertips encountered the coarse hair between her legs did caution overrule his arousal.

'We should stop,' he whispered. 'Your father would not be pleased to learn of this.'

'Why does my father have to know?'

Most likely he would be drunk at this hour. Nathaniel knew him only slightly but he trusted Susannah's account. Her father, who proclaimed with such conviction his hatred of tyranny, was entirely blind to his own. He had lost two brothers in the war and not even the King's death had assuaged him. It was his rage which engendered the welt on Susannah's cheek. 'People will be wondering where we are,' said Nathaniel.

'Let them wonder.'

She gripped his wrist to prevent him drawing away. He could not think of an adequate gesture to console her and absolve himself. A pat on the cheek would only rouse her fury (she was no child), which sight he both feared and adored. Lifting his arm, with her hand still attached to it, he kissed her knuckles. 'Come,' he said sweetly. 'Thomas will have food for us.'

Propitiated and, he expected, hungry (for she had worked hard all day), Susannah followed him, closely at first and then at a respectable distance, back down the path. As they emerged from the bracken, Nathaniel listened to the intermittent churring of nightjars, or goat-suckers as the Diggers called them. He reminded himself to set a trap so that he might study one and commit it to paper. A scythe of wings overhead made him flinch; Susannah, he saw, was not troubled. She flapped a lazy hand at a moon-bright moth, which promptly ascended to the nightjar's path. He stopped to see whether the moth would get eaten; but he lost sight of it and Susannah clucked her tongue to signal her impatience. They pressed on and Nathaniel wondered, as smoke from the nearest fire began to tickle his throat, where the birds came from in the springtime. Did they hibernate in sand, as swallows in mud, to rise again with the sun? And how did they manage to hide all day, when the heath was filled with people?

'What are you thinking?' asked Susannah with a smiling voice.

'About the birds. Where they come from. Where they go.'

'What do you care, so long as *they* know?' She skipped a few paces ahead of him. 'Oh, Nat, walk faster. I'm famished with your talking.'

Quickening his pace to placate her, he returned to thoughts that had begun to plague him. Others did not see the world as he saw it. His affinity for this dry brooding landscape was not shared by his . . . what? Hosts? Companions? They saw only food and shelter where he saw beauty: God's art.

Two months earlier, as he approached the settlement on St George's Hill (only days before the local gentry, using hired muscle, had pushed the Diggers east to Cobham), the huts and hardy cattle and scattering of furze-cutters at their song had been dwarfed in his mind by the land itself. For one accustomed to green pastures and the wooded fleece of the weald, this was a low, sun-baked, thorny place, primordial in its languor, where squat shadows crouched, like drought-stricken toads, under the juiceless heathers, and the sky, instead of the familiar and gentle canopy, seemed an oppressive mass of rainless clouds, taunting men with its withheld gifts and crushing them with its grandeur. How could he not relish the challenge of painting such a place?

His trepidation mounting, he had pressed on towards the common. He sank waist deep into bracken, then emerged to a sward of grass furrowed by the wind's fingers. Banks of ling threw out, at his approach, small twittering birds that settled on branches to spy on him. Then a cry went up from the lookouts and the Diggers came to meet him.

Nathaniel was glad that he had changed his clothes. Having bequeathed to the tavern in Weybridge his velvet jacket and swapped his hat for a labourer's beehive, he found to his satisfaction that he was dressed much like another man. The furze-cutters dropped their billhooks to greet him; and instead of hostile suspicion – still the norm in weary England – he was met with handshakes, warm smiles, addressed as *brother*. A few eyes noted his imperfect disguise, the cravat and, under the waistcoat, still-white linen; but since he intended to paint in these clothes, he knew they would soon be spattered. Then there would be no way to tell him apart.

His equipment looked out of place, however, and like his accent he could not conceal it. The Diggers gaped to hear his ambitions. He would paint what? Some looked almost offended when, currying favour, he asserted that *they* would be his subject.

'We are here to live,' said one, 'and must labour to live.'

Nathaniel's pledge, hastily adopted, to contribute to the enterprise met with scepticism. Then a young man stepped through the furze-cutters. His face was reassuring; it was not gnarled or mangled like so many that surrounded him. It was Nathaniel's first glimpse of Thomas. The apothecary smiled and placed a hand on his shoulder. 'The light,' he said, 'is shining on this heath and Providence may want it remembered. We cannot trust our instincts when God is at work. Let our guest prove his skills and then we may decide.'

So Nathaniel had sat down in the dry grass and sketched, with a nervous hand, a finger-sucking toddler who watched from the crowd. The sketch soared from hand to hand, like a bird trying to elude its captors, and a common vote was carried that Nathaniel could stay.

The young man who had spoken for him became his guide. Where had they come from, these brave, defiant people? From Kent and Sussex and Surrey, escaping greedy landlords and unforgiving creditors; or else from London and its surrounding towns, coming in search of a life, if not easier, then closer at least to justice and to God. Nathaniel admired them for their eloquence, though few of them could read. They were ingenious at collecting water (it tasted like old lant) where to his eyes there seemed none, and they made clever shelters out of fragile materials. They knew, from experience, all the properties of the heath. Though their children were often hungry and walked on bare feet, though the women looked pinched and shapeless at thirty, yet the pride of these Diggers, the certainty that God approved of their actions, shone in their eyes like nobility. There were no leaders. Each man and woman spoke freely and was heard. They worked and prayed in unison and looked for redemption in this harsh and ancient garden: fallen Eden, whose fruits were sharp and bitter.

Susannah called out when she discovered her friends. 'Hey, brothers! Ho!'

They were sprawling, replete after supper, about the cold ashes of a cooking fire in a small, sandy depression backed by mature heather. Nathaniel returned their easy hand signals, still marvelling at his licence to stroll, unguarded and at night, with a virgin half his age.

Susannah revealed her plump legs as she leapt into the sand and fell to the remaining oast cakes. 'Toby found honey,' she exclaimed as Nathaniel, wearing a diffident smile, sought a place to sit. There was light enough from the gibbous moon and from surrounding campfires for him to see his neighbours. Toby Corbet, who did not trust him, was there; Nathaniel's friend Thomas; also John and Margaret, with their child wrapped in sackcloth, her face swollen from teething.

'Toby raided a bees' nest.'

'Hive,' corrected Thomas, who was paring his fingernails.

'Did the bees not sting you?'

Toby Corbet shook his head and gathered a quantity of pipe smoke in his mouth, which he released slowly, in demonstration of his method. 'Baffled 'em with smoke. Makes 'em dozy. Easy then. Trick is not to get greedy.' His hooded eyes flashed at Nathaniel, then returned to Susannah. 'Let me put a drop on your oast cake.'

Nathaniel looked away as, like a good spaniel, she

fell to her knees to take honey from Toby Corbet's hand.

'Where did you go?' asked Thomas.

'To the hill, to watch the sun set. It makes the gorse flicker as if it were on fire . . . if you catch it at the right moment.'

('How does that please you?'

'*Mm*.')

'You did not take your paintbox with you.'

'He was not gone to paint,' said Margaret with a wink. Nathaniel accepted a flagon from her husband to quench his thirst and anger. He would have to watch Susannah with Toby Corbet; she could not be conceded to that woodsman and his sour, mistrustful grin. At the same time he was troubled to think of obligations that he might be incurring.

'Did you read the pamphlet I gave you?'

Nathaniel's face was a blank. He saw the handsome, sunburned face of the young apothecary. He recognised the hope and affection that illuminated it, the intelligence also.

'The Winstanley,' said Thomas, clarifying.

'Lord, he's read it to *us* enough times.' This was Corbet, dipping another cake in his handkerchief. 'You are lucky, *brother*. You have only to hear it in your head.'

Thomas, accustomed to his friend's coarse manner, offered a two-fingered response and then turned serious. 'We need men of learning,' he said, 'and artists, who can speak for us in the world of power. You think it nonsense but Winstanley is our Baptist—'

'Words cannot help us.'

'—preparing the world for our enterprise.' Thomas recited from memory: '*Why may we not have our heaven here (that is, a comfortable livelihood on earth) and heaven hereafter too?*'

'Because,' said Corbet, licking his fingers, 'men like him will not allow it.'

Nathaniel saw the elbow jerked in his direction and reared indignantly to his knees. 'That is false and you know it. I served our freedom's cause—'

'You never so much as fired a shot.'

'There are many ways of fighting, Mr Corbet.'

'Did you throw mud?'

Susannah gaped on the argument, her mouth a mortar of broken food.

'I worked as a pamphleteer,' said Nathaniel. 'My services were freely offered . . .'

'So *that*'s how we won.'

Nathaniel bit his tongue. He had heard of Toby Corbet's desertion from the New Model Army. Fiery speakers, zealous to turn the world upside down, had roused a good number of infantrymen. The Day of Revelation was at hand, they said, and the old order would crumble. Meantime they, the flower of England, killed and were killed; one kind of tyranny would fall; but when the soldiers returned, whole or in part, to their ageing wives and hungry children, not one would be more free or prosperous than if the King had lived.

'Do not be angry with me, friend.' Nathaniel tried to sound conciliatory. 'I came here to learn from you. I have nothing to teach. And I see the value of what you are doing.'

'You would not see it so kindly, Mr Deller, if we were camped at your door.'

'I *have* no door. My father is dead. My brother has the estate and I am disgusted with London.'

'Oh, heed the martyr.'

Thomas threw a fistful of sand between them, as though parting dogs. Corbet blinked in surprise. 'Enough,' said Thomas. 'Nathaniel is our friend and loyal to the cause. You have no reason to quarrel with him.'

'Not when danger is so near.' This was Margaret. The teething infant in her arms was awake and threatening to gibber. 'And we have so many new mouths to feed.'

'That,' said Corbet, 'is one more reason to dispense with *him*.'

'Be silent,' said Nathaniel, his imperious manner, which he had striven to conceal, escaping. 'Margaret is right. If we must argue, let us do it tomorrow and at our leisure.'

Lying down on his side, with hands tucked between his knees, Toby Corbet presented his rump to the company. 'Only *you* have leisure,' he muttered.

There was no responding to this. Nathaniel looked at the sullen posture of the woodsman (perhaps the rumours, which buzzed like gnats about the settlement, of soldiers near by had put a deserter's fear in him). It was true that he, Nathaniel, was excused the hardest labours. Upon his arrival, he had set about winning the Diggers over to his art; and once it became obvious, through his earnest attempts, that he had neither skill nor stamina to work all day with the livestock, or to make shelters for the community, he was tolerated in his difference. It pleased the women to have a gentleman on the heath: one who had seen the new light shining yet retained his old-fashioned airs and graces.

Mostly, though, it was the children who vouched for him. They liked to watch him at work, and he let them turn the pages of his notebook. Sometimes, at their entreaty, he would paint their faces, making them shriek with merriment as they searched for rain-fallen mirrors. To the older ones he spoke of the Nieuwe Doolhof, the pleasure gardens of Amsterdam, and described the curious objects to be found in his tutor's studio. He made sketches, for the children to keep, of the stuffed civets on their crumbling log, and the stinking fox that seemed alive, so well had the artisan done his work. He painted, in affectionate remembrance of his tutor, Keyser's bronze inkwell in the shape of a dolphin – his statuettes of elephants and lions – busts of blind Homer and Seneca – a torso of Venus unearthed near Rome – and a Turkish scimitar dented (so Keyser liked to claim) in the course of its encounter with a crusader's skull.

Through innocence, then, he gained acceptance among the adults. Yet he knew that Toby Corbet was not alone in distrusting him. His vocabulary, his manners, even his clothes (though they were dirty and worn now) set him apart. When the Diggers laughed he was unsure of the jest and opened his mouth, or bared his teeth, in a dumb show of mirth. Though he was one of the few able to read, the communal Bible never came to his hands for the evening Scripture. The Diggers preferred one of their own – a ginger troll with a perpetually wet lower lip – to read haltingly, with a black finger ploughing the page, than to hear Nathaniel's swift and mellifluous recitation. (Thomas, too, could read aloud; yet he seemed to know and to accept, with a serenity that Nathaniel could not muster, that *his* tasks on the heath lay elsewhere.) Nathaniel, when doubts assailed him, imagined a secret language of nods and sighs and loaded glances from which he was excluded. He had come to Surrey seeking innocents who would admire his craft; he had come to live with honest men of a kind extinct in the city; yet he was not of their party.

One evening, when Toby Corbet and Will Tanner and one-eyed former sergeant Hale were chewing coney pie in the meeting-hut, Nathaniel had tried to join their conversation. Were the Diggers not satisfied, he asked, to see the tyrant beheaded and True Religion triumph?

'Our lot will change little,' came the reply. 'This war was a victory for freeholders and they will hold on to their advantages.'

'But surely things have improved for all Englishmen?'

'We will have no tenant rights . . .' Sergeant Hale fixed a reproachful eye on Nathaniel. 'The enclosures have deprived us even of our poor livelihoods. They have made us beggars and vagabonds. And each justice in every parish has us whipped for our misfortunes.'

The memory of this encounter pursued Nathaniel as, feeling obscurely ashamed, he left his companions and wandered across the heather. He looked back and saw the young parents lying with the moaning child sucking on Margaret's knuckle. Toby Corbet, knocked out on cheap rum, was already snoring. Susannah sat, neglected and digesting, at his side.

Kind, impulsive Thomas waded after him through the tall heather. 'Nathaniel,' he said, 'do not be offended. You are his rival for the girl's affections. And further advanced in them, I dare say.'

'Is that what troubles him?'

'What else?'

'Oh, come. We have all heard the rumours. Things may seem calm now but there is a sense of foreboding.'

Thomas shook his head, smiling. 'We are stronger than you think. There are more of us every day.'

'You are not loved by those with the power to stop you. This morning a family arrived from Ashtead. They saw soldiers on the road three miles away.'

'So?'

'This may be their destination.'

Thomas pursed his lips. He had served on Parliament's side as apothecary-surgeon. He refused to believe it. 'Many of us here were soldiers. Many of us fought. If the army is near by, it will be composed of good, common men with whom we prayed and suffered.'

'They will follow their orders.'

Thomas was impatient of these presentiments. Playfully he plucked at Nathaniel's elbow. 'You are not going to sleep in the hut,' he said. 'Come back, please. It is such a warm night that we may sleep in the open.' He grinned mischievously. 'Susannah,' he said, 'will be waiting for you.'

'I am persuaded.'

They clambered through ling as dry as catgut back to the clearing. Susannah lay, abandoned, on her side, and seemed unaware of her lover's return. Or else she slept. Thomas, like a cat trying to settle, crawled about until he found a position that pleased him; whereupon he made a pillow out of his jacket and lay down to sleep.

Nathaniel stretched out on his back, with one arm behind his head, and looked up at the cold, blinking stars.

Lying there he recalled, with some of the pang of homesickness, his tutor's house in the Lauriergracht. Nicolaes Keyser had been too honest to conceal the rot in his studio walls. That fissured plaster made its way even into his paintings. Such mould and moisture – a different planet to this brittle heath in parched summer. Fastening shut his eyes, Nathaniel returned in memory to Amsterdam: a city of ghosts in winter, when mist stole over everything, in summer a monstrous stink, the canals clogged with ordure and every pretty face hidden in a handkerchief or pomander.

None of these things seemed to trouble his tutor, whose nose, like the rest of him, lacked pretension. Nicolaes Keyser was a portraitist, unable, in his own words, to compete with the history painters of Antwerp or Italy. His consolation was a most unflinching eye. Nathaniel smiled at the stars to consider how, but for the Calvinist disdain for affectation (a most displayable virtue), Nicolaes Keyser would long ago have died of indigence; for he recorded every flaw and blemish in a face, regarding these not as corruptions of the true, or Platonic, features but rather as individuating marks, the outward traces of a life, hieroglyphs that shape a soul. It was a painter's task to seek the *essence*: that which makes a thing unique. No tree, he would contend, is like another. This paving stone has different stains to its neighbour and has not endured the same injuries. When not philosophising on dross and macules, the old man would haunt the city's estate auctions, able to buy few prints but copying, in pen and brown ink, more expensive works before they found a buyer. Thus Nathaniel came to know van Leyden and Goltzius and the Fleming Rubens. Nicolaes Keyser, for all that he admired these works, lamented the lack of soul in their subjects. These were people, he said, who had never trod on earth.

So Nathaniel copied his tutor and parroted his philosophy, until through emulation his hand found its own rhythm, his mind its own preoccupations, and Keyser began to praise his studies done after life – *naer het leven*. It was a strange training of immeasurable value. Nathaniel learned that, every moment, he might kick up gold from the dust of life. He was instructed to go on long walks, armed with pennies

and a sketchbook, about the city and its environs –
saving something of what he saw.

Nathaniel remembered one afternoon when his
observations had been shattered by the barking of
muskets. It was Sunday, a good day for wildfowling,
and he was beginning to regret, with every flinch-
inducing shot, the dank shelter of his garret, when a
copse of willows shook in front of him and a preacher
almost ran him down in his haste to collect a dead
bittern from his hunting dog's jaws. Listening now to
the nightjars' whirr, Nathaniel recalled how this
Sabbath massacre had displeased him. He had
looked, making polite and insincere noises of admiration, at the splayed, straw-and-tawny fan of feathers,
at the chequered pattern of the bittern's breast and its
sharp dishonoured beak. He wanted to buy the bird,
to restore it in watercolour and oils; but the preacher
was boasting already about his supper, while his
fingers plucked at downy feathers. Trudging back
to higher ground, Nathaniel had brooded: even so
transient are our joys, as birds on the wing . . .

He was shaken and restored to the present by the
baby's cries. Some abrupt pain must have woken her,
for there was barely an interlude between the first
moan and this desperate howling. Nathaniel opened
his eyes. The moon was engulfed in cloud. He saw the
parents sit up, John trying to dandle while Margaret
unbuttoned. The others lay in obdurate stillness, save

Thomas, who, to judge by the alacrity of his movements, must have been awake beforehand; for he crawled to join the family on his hands and knees, and Nathaniel heard snatches of a muted consultation. Eventually the child stopped crying, though possessed by shivering spasms and hiccups. Nathaniel turned on to his side, his face in the warm crook of his arm, and tried to think his way back to the past; which, for being gone, seemed a happy country.

He recreated the chamber where he used to dine with his tutor and Mrs Keyser. His host was always, even in the last days, *sir*, but his hostess, as soon as Nathaniel began to merit her husband's good opinion, insisted on being called Griet. She was marvellously ugly, with a fishwife's halitosis, and Nicolaes Keyser adored her (which proved, if nothing else, that he was no hypocrite). And it was true that, with familiarity, her prognathous jaw softened and her chestnut eyes emerged, with all their liveliness and humour, from the mottled misadventure of her face. The good *huysvrou* became most dear to Nathaniel, not least on account of Keyser's adoration of her. She had borne him seven children, four of whom still lived, all within walking distance of the parental home.

Griet Keyser had wept bitterly at the news of Nathaniel's departure, while her husband, having exhausted himself in vain attempts to dissuade his pupil, sat on his chair in an attitude of profound despondency. Oh, Nathaniel itched to be in England when his art was yet untutored. Keyser showed him *Les Misères de la Guerre* to discourage him. But it was England that he wished to see. He was tired of the flatness of Amsterdam, where corpses of cows floated in the canals and the stink of the tanneries almost drove him mad. Keyser thought he *had* lost his wits. He himself had fought, and was injured, at the siege of 's-Hertogenbosch.

There was no glory in battle, he used to say. Could violence really bind up a wound in society? What commonwealth could prosper when it was built on the bones of the dead?

Fired by the pamphlets of exiled patriots, Nathaniel had invoked freedom and true religion.

'You are a fool,' Keyser interrupted. 'Extreme remedies replace distemper with disaster. They kill the disease by killing the patient.' He recalled, for instances, the long Flemish wars, the unholy rages of the Duke of Alva and the ravages wrought in Germany since before Nathaniel was born. 'We are too few in number who will not countenance the shedding of blood for a *credo*. I have seen how easily truces, stitched by moderates, may be picked apart by zealots. Then greedy princes wrap themselves in the bloody threads. You, my boy, would do far better to go to Rome and continue learning. You must be one who works to *mend* the world. Pragmatism and toleration, no matter what the priests say, are most blessed in the sight of God.'

Back then, with the schooner that would take him to Harwich lilting at the docks, Nathaniel had barely heeded this wisdom. He needed to witness war for himself before he could come, by slow degrees, to the same conclusions.

As much as the hope and disorder, as much as the sight of soldiers dipping providential fingers in their Bibles, playing cards or sleeping, haggard with fear or exhausted by boredom, it had been the corpses which held his attention. Of course, he had seen the dead before, his mother and his grandparents, but they had been composed for burial, dressed in cerements with their faces powdered and their jaws tightly bound. There had been decorum in those hands irrefrangibly clasped; their postures looked not untenable. With the war dead, it was different. They were, for the most part, contorted, their legs horribly folded and their arms awry. The cavernous nostrils, the closed eyes of his loved ones had threatened, in his innocent fancy, to flare and open. It was impossible to believe this of the soldier's black snout and his dusty eye with its paper lid. Nathaniel believed, unshakeably, that the soul exists, that some essence returns to God when the vessel of the body is broken. He had tried, as an act of piety, to capture the vacancy of once-inhabited faces, to record the cheek that might have inspired a lover's caress before it turned an inhuman colour. He could convey, well enough, what remained of these men; but how to suggest what had fled?

Every soldier acknowledged the fallen, whether his own or the enemy's, with mute respect. For all the savagery of battle (whose aftermath was chiefly what Nathaniel saw of it), the mutilation of corpses was regarded with horror. That putrescent mess – went each man's thoughts – might be your cousin or uncle. Tomorrow it could well be *you*.

Nathaniel remembered following Roundheads near Oxford when groans of dismay spread through the ranks. A magpie was plucking eye-flesh from a fallen sheep in a field. The sheep, to judge from its feeble lamentations, was still alive. Without orders from the captain, a musket was fired. No punishment followed. Three days later, as crows began to settle after a skirmish, young victors ran hollering through the shambled field, intent on saving their dead comrades' eyes.

It was too raw to think about. Nathaniel, trying not to heed the present whimpering of the baby, thought his way back to the war's aftermath.

He had done Parliament some service. His father forgave him for abandoning his studies. But he refused to return to Amsterdam. It was time for life, in the shadow of so much death, to begin . . .

There followed his journeyman days in Lambeth: living on his father's munificence while he designed tapestries for Mortlake and made copies of other men's paintings. He was kept busy in this way throughout the King's trial and its astounding outcome. A thundering head cold kept him away from the Whitehall scaffold; but no illness could block his ears to the visionaries who saw, with the beheading, auguries of the New Jerusalem. Unaccompanied by his more politic friends, he went to hear Ranters and Levellers as they announced, in the crowded streets, changes beyond all comprehension.

Troubled and roused by these speakers, Nathaniel had sounded out their ideas with Mr Deller. Even as life fell away from him, his ailing father dwelt on the future. He doubted the wisdom of a republic. As for those hotheads advocating a new order, 'If they have their way,' he said, 'the needy of England will rise up against the gentry and all order will be confounded.'

Was it a betrayal of his father's convictions when Nathaniel, newly orphaned, locked up his lodgings and undertook this journey to the common?

His stomach pained him and he passed wind. It was shame gnawing at his innards. And yet he had been right, abundantly right, after Jeake the commissioner had sneered at so much beauty, to find refuge on this heath. Between mercantile contempt and courtly vanity, where could true art prosper? Here it meant nothing; so the people might yet be brought to it with judgements unclouded. The Diggers, Nathaniel hoped, would experience beauty as children do, wholeheartedly and without prejudice.

And he? He would discover his subject. An art shaped by the new England, where every thing merits attention. The land would be the wellspring of a native genius. Starting in this second Eden, he would dig, as it were, with his brushes, under the surface of things.

'Wuu. *Wuuu* . . .'

Failing to ease their child's distress, the parents despaired of sleeping. Nathaniel heard them whisper (needlessly, since the girl's lamentations kept everyone awake) and then rise, taking their mewling bundle into the deep heather. The others, relieved of the disturbance, sighed and resettled. Nathaniel took in the quiet air. He was conscious of nausea in his stomach. This was dog-tiredness, which only sleep could help. Let it come. Vanish, thoughts. Tomorrow will bring matter enough.

He wakened slightly, his lust also, when Susannah came, with sleepy breath, to rest her head on his shoulder. He refrained from touching her. Instead he feigned deep sleep; and heard, most distantly, so that he could not be certain whether he was dreaming already, the unquenchable cries of a child.

'Cold?'

Nathaniel opened his eyes and grimaced. He ruffled his hair. Susannah had left him.

'What time is it?'

Thomas shrugged and tossed him a crust of bread. Nathaniel, propping himself on his elbows, found the dawn already advanced. The temperature must have dropped in the small hours, for William Shaw and another man, whom Nathaniel did not recognise, were starting a new fire among the cold ashes. Smoke whispered from the unknown man's hands. He cupped them, like one inspecting a captive mouse, and gently blew. Then he leaned towards the kindling and released the flame.

Nathaniel sat up, with pleasure, to watch. Before he came to the common he had never seen gorse burn. It was as if the plant had been made of fire – fire stilled, distilled and crystallised in the sharp green thorns – and the furze-cutters, when they dropped a brand into those frozen flames, thawed them suddenly. For the gorse shivered, crackled and dissolved. The heat was intense, the gorse whistled, and then barely ashes stood out on the pyre.

With the kindling alight, the men fed the fire more substantial fuel, which for all the late dryness crackled and wheezed. There was a smell of cooking oats from a more advanced fire. Nathaniel's mouth watered.

'What have you planned for today?' asked Thomas, who was working beside him with a pestle and mortar.

'Landscapes.'

'From the hill?'

Nathaniel nodded and peered askance at the medicinal paste. Was it for the baby's gums? he wondered.

'I ought to warn you about the trees.' Thomas did not look up from his pounding.

'What trees?'

'Oh, you know. The oaks by the river.'

They were magnificent: five ancients that might have been acorns when Alfred fought the Danes. Nathaniel had admired them on their first day in Cobham, when others were busy erecting shelters or feeding the livestock. In his own hut, which he shared with the apothecary, he had several bistre-and-chalk drawings of them. Indeed, they were to feature in his painting that morning.

'What is being done to them?'

'A meeting was held last night, while you were strolling with your mistress.'

'She is not my mistress.'

'The truth is that we need fuel. And the best timber may fetch a good price on the market.'

'I'll wager this was Corbet's idea.' Nathaniel stood up, though his cramped legs were not ready and he felt himself falter.

'Be careful, Nat. A vote was carried and you may not stop it.'

This seemed to Nathaniel a damned impertinence. Having abjured possessions, it was not the Diggers' decision to make. 'They are so handsome,' he protested. 'So few still stand of that age.' Striding towards the river, he tried to outpace his friend.

'Nathaniel, be reasonable. You see how our numbers grow. So do our needs. For generations, common land has been shrinking and now people must take refuge where they can.'

'They do not have to destroy them. A few dead branches can be spared but not the trees themselves.'

'You make no sense.'

Soon they reached the copse, whence sounds of industry drifted on the breeze. 'We are only passing through,' said Nathaniel, '*they* remain across the generations. Let me speak to them.'

'We have need of the wood! Oh, for pity's sake . . .' Nathaniel marched implacably on. 'Brother, you have no authority to challenge the common will.'

'May I not protest?'

'You may,' said Thomas. His attempt to sound conciliatory made Nathaniel feel churlish, a prating actor, even as outrage boiled inside him. 'But it will do no good. You know very well that your credit here is uncertain. Some of the Diggers mistrust you.'

'Without reason.'

'I *mean* mistrust . . . They suspect you for a spy.' This made Nathaniel halt. 'You do not belong among the dispossessed and they cannot understand why you should *wish* to. Our freedom entails many duties. The commoners' needs are paramount and if you protest against their necessity, those libels will seem to be confirmed.'

Grudgingly, Nathaniel saw sense. He nodded and, at a slower and more resigned pace, continued towards the trees. 'Do not fret,' he said. 'I will make no sound, I promise.'

Nobody greeted him as he entered the shifting green shade. The first of the five oaks was under assault. Its trunk, distended with age and cankers, was a maze for ants, each scale of bark an inch thick; there was a gaping, cauterised hole halfway up which must have served generations of owls. For all its decrepitude, the tree's rambling branches still boasted an abundance of tender leaves. To facilitate its fall, the Diggers had lopped the greatest branches. Their sons and nephews, lean and strong, were hacking at the foliage with billhooks.

'How long,' Nathaniel asked one of the lads, trying to sound amiable, 'how long before it falls, would you say?'

There was no human answer. The oak tree groaned like a dying god; its belly was hacked and oozing. After five more minutes a cry went up from the work leader. Nathaniel recognised Toby Corbet. The woodsman ordered boys to join the men on the ropes and bring the great tree down. Meanwhile the axe-men continued, grimacing as woodchip flew, to scoop away at the heartwood. Nathaniel hoped the other trees might be spared long enough for him to paint them. He sat down beside a coppiced hazel overrun by honeysuckle and waited for the tree to die. Soon enough it surrendered with a mighty whistle and a snapping as of bones. After the thunder of collapse, amid billowing clouds of dust and leaves, the Diggers whooped for joy as though a tyrant's statue had been toppled.

Nathaniel walked up to the raw, splintered stump and found, at its centre, black rottenness. He tried to count the rings of grain while the crew rested and drank cider. Seeing him point and move his lips, Toby Corbet mocked: 'It's called a *tree*, Mr Deller.'

He emerged from the copse on a breeze of derision. Thomas was waiting for him. They walked to their hut.

'How old was it?'

'I do not know,' said Nathaniel.

In the hut he assembled his drawing paper, his freshly whittled pen and ink bottle, his brushes and paintbox and the copy of van Mander's *Schilder-boek* that served as a board for working on. Thomas arranged on his mattress a number of potions; then sat down to mould the paste in his mortar. There was a scrabbling outside. Nathaniel was disappointed when a boy, not Susannah, appeared at the entrance.

'What is the matter, Samuel?'

'Please . . .' The boy was fighting for breath, his thin arms flapping about his ribs. 'The baby.'

Without another word, Thomas flung some vials into his bag and left the hut. He took the boy's hand; but Samuel was too weak to run and Thomas hauled him on to his back.

When they had gone, Nathaniel set out with his implements across the heath, through last night's tunnel of bracken and gorse, back to his sketching post.

He surveyed the scene and found in himself no desire to work, to create form on a void of paper. Instead he felt a baser longing. It was, he knew from experience, often thus. When the creative impulse fails, the body seeks the consolation of sensual release. He wondered how many bastards owed their lives to this confusion of lust with a finer desire for creation. He wondered also, with roving eyes, where Susannah might be. For the present at least Toby Corbet was occupied: there was one advantage of his tree-felling.

He laid the book on his lap and unfastened the clasp on his watercolour box. Burrowing under the partial shelter of birch saplings, he gazed south across

Surrey. He sketched for a time not the scene before him but what he could remember of Susannah's face. The shape of her cheeks and her plump, almost excessive lips came easily enough; but either his memory or his talent foundered on her eyes. What colour were they? Had he ever studied them closely?

He turned the page over and began to paint the common, with its doomed copse of oaks (now partly bald) and the sinuous beam of the river. After a time of mechanical effort, the creative trance began. He breathed through his mouth as in slumber. The spell transferred itself to the blotches on the page.

Wet spots appeared on the paper. Nathaniel looked up, with a taut jaw, at the massed but too-bright clouds. A feeble mizzle was falling, negligible in quantity, like the passing overhead of incontinent insects. Nathaniel extended his palm to catch a stinging droplet. He was in this begging attitude when Thomas joined him.

'What news?'

Thomas's normally jovial expression was grim and thunderous. 'I should have told her not to do it. I have known children die from such attention.'

'Good Lord, what has happened?'

'Margaret's baby is teething.'

'Yes, I know.'

'And in some discomfort, as is often the case.' Thomas thumped himself on the thigh. 'It makes no sense. The practice outlasts all evidence and reason.' He met Nathaniel's questioning gaze. 'She lanced the child's gums,' he explained.

'That is bad?'

'Well, now she has a fever. And I fear it may worsen.'

'But your potion—'

'Children at that age have not the wit to be credulous.'

Nathaniel could think of nothing to say. It was the first time he had seen his friend despairing.

'And *you* worry for your trees,' Thomas said reproachfully; then swiftly apologised. He produced from the folds of his apron two, somewhat crushed, flead cakes. 'I am forever hungry,' he said.

Nathaniel bit into the cake offered to him. It was stale and the pig's membrane inside was an unsightly grey. Still they munched, glad to have something to line their stomachs.

Nathaniel watched his young friend obliquely, while Thomas gazed across the heath. A breeze ruffled his straight dark hair but he did not stroke it back into place. There was no vanity in the boy. Nathaniel had recognised his passion, though, the day they met: a shared temperament at the root of their understanding. Pledged to his ideals – to a world without caste or property – Thomas might have been a dour companion. But hope kept his manner light.

Of his baser, or more universal, longings Nathaniel knew nothing. Thomas seemed untroubled by desire, or else it was absorbed by his devotion to the colony.

'Does it pay well, painting?'

Nathaniel was surprised by the question. 'There is good money,' he said, 'if one is ready to flatter.' Nicolaes Keyser in Amsterdam could ask fifty guilders, per sitter, for a group portrait. Nathaniel chose to keep this information to himself. 'But wealth is not my concern. I mean to become a learned painter – *pictor doctus*. One useful to his fellow men.'

'Ah.'

Nathaniel went on, though unbidden, to describe his methods: how he sketched on foot, as it were, always carrying his tablet and silverpoint to put down a sight, which he perfected later in pen and brush. 'A man does not learn to see by forever staying in his house. Always observe. Remember Aristotle. Art loves chance and chance loves art.'

'So you draw everything? Anything?'

'That I have a mind to. And as long as it exists in God's creation.'

'A fly, for instance?'

'In Holland there are painters who grow rich on flies. Along with snails and moths and flowers.'

'Not very lofty.'

'Just as you have said, Thomas, concerning Our

Lord. We must go through our own senses and ignore, if need be, the traditions of men. What we cannot see and feel must go unpainted.'

'What of cherubs, then, and your bonny Venus?'

'They are not mine.'

Thomas seemed to take this in. Pensively he picked at the shreds in his teeth. 'What is *your* subject?'

'My Dutch tutor would have told me to forswear all this.' Nathaniel gestured at the sweltering heath, at the commoners toiling in its sand and dust. ' "Ignore the world and your fellow men. Go to Rome, my boy." '

Thomas stared with eyes alight. For a moment he forgot about the popish Antichrist. 'You could have gone to *Rome*?'

'To acquire all the mannerisms of the age? To paint mythological whores and heroes? No, Thomas, in *this* place I pitch my temple.' Filthy children, breechless, waved at them from the plain, revealing their teeth. There was a smell of baked sand and wood smoke and cattle dung. A yaffle passed in a flash of woodsman green. 'To cover the world in art,' said Nathaniel. 'To store it on canvas for safe-keeping. That seems a sacred task.'

'Can you draw me?'

'You?'

Thomas blushed like a schoolboy. 'It is my vanity . . .'

'I should be happy to.'

'Truly? Ought I not to change my clothes?'

'Let me set you down as you are. As the Lord sees you.'

Thomas glanced up at the sky. 'I hope He will forgive me.'

'This is no sin.'

Nathaniel set the unfinished painting on the sand, with flints on each corner to keep it from absconding, and as he prepared a clean paper he felt his enthusiasm for the work returning. Thomas was *actual* for him, while those trees perhaps were merely symbols. He made his first mark on the page.

'What must I do now?'

'Sit calmly. Do nothing, or as you please.'

'May I read?' From the bulging flaps of his apron Thomas extracted a small, black leather prayer book. Nathaniel had never seen it before. Was he to be vouchsafed a glimpse of private devotions?

'Sit over there, would you, by that tree.'

'A very paltry thing.'

Another oak. Slowly, even in this sandy ground, it had consolidated and grown; but not to the splendour of its cousins on the plain. 'I will make a better job of you,' said Nathaniel, 'for having it in the background.'

Thomas wrinkled his nose at the tree. 'The New Republic,' he declared, 'a nascent and starveling thing.' He sat down, extended his legs, and began to remove his tattered straw hat.

'No, cover your head,' said Nathaniel.

'With *this* cow's breakfast?'

'Please, I would put it in.' Nathaniel bit his cheeks gently, as he always did when he began a picture. With a thin piece of charcoal he traced an outline of his friend and the leaf spray behind him. When he was satisfied that he had found the predestined lines, he dipped his pen in the inkpot. Thomas began to fidget. He lifted a buttock to see whether he was sitting on ants. He blew into his prayer book to dislodge sand or some pious gnat. 'Tell me about your master,' said Nathaniel, with the precise calm and ulterior motive of a consulting physician. 'Without gesticulating.'

'My master?' Thomas puffed out his cheeks in consideration. 'He volunteered to serve in the New Model Army. The King's men had all the surgeons and physicians.'

'And you went with him.'

'Yes.'

'With your father's consent?'

'He was dead.'

'Mine too now.' Nathaniel, engaged in shadowing the eyes, did not look up. 'Was he a good man?'

'My father?'

'The apothecary.'

'Well, he believed in all his remedies. That made it easier for him to administer them.'

This was the second sour note from Thomas. Nathaniel feared he would be distracted from his drawing if he probed this wound of doubt. 'But you did not fight yourself,' he said.

'My master died in a fall from his horse. I continued his work. Patching up wounds. I never fired a shot but I had to fish for a few in men's bellies.'

There was his bitterness again. 'And then you came here.'

'Where else would I be? I had heard about the Diggers back in Lambeth and thought, No good will come out of Parliament.'

'Why do you say so?'

'Because the Galenist physicians retain all their power. Improvement is scotched in the world. Nine out of ten suffer and their suffering is neglected. Meantime the wealth of England is not commonly shared.'

Nathaniel regretted having summoned this anger; it was distorting the apothecary's face, predicting future wrinkles. 'But here things are different, are they not? I know you spurn kind words as flattery, Thomas, but I admire your devotion to the health of the commoners.'

'They are my brothers and sisters in Christ. The needle's eye will not prove too great an obstacle for them. Out there' – he gestured across the heath, – 'is natural humility. Princes could learn from it. And preachers too.'

'Amen.'

'There is an absolute virtue in poverty which Christ taught and has been forgotten.'

Nathaniel nodded. Inwardly he thought: If the least of your brothers had property, he would behave like those you despise.

For a long time they sat in silence, but for the scratching of Nathaniel's pen. Thomas looked at his book and turned the pages faster, surely, than he could read them. Both men, for different reasons, feigned not to hear a second oak crashing to the ground.

Then it was Thomas's turn to ask a question.

'What brought you out here?'

Nathaniel stopped to pick a fibre from his nib. 'Curiosity,' he said. 'And I suppose anger.'

'Against the unjust world?'

'At the contempt shown for painting. The dead King's collection—'

'For *what*?'

'I saw it, Thomas. I had the chance to visit Whitehall as the guest of a commissioner. One appointed to appraise and sell the goods, as he called them.'

'And for *that* you came here?'

Nathaniel understood his friend's incredulity. He had not yet spoken of his encounter with the salesman who bandied prices for the priceless and never guessed its value. 'The man's name was Jeake.'

'Jeake?'

'I cornered him in the alehouse. I bought him porter and a lamb's-tail pie . . .'

'Oh, mercy,' said Thomas, gripping his belly.

'In return for which I was granted a tour of the works for sale.'

Though most likely a man of feeble fancy, Valentine Jeake had imagined with scornful relish the dead King competing with Buckingham ('his father's whore') and my Lord of Arundel to squander the nation's wealth. Nathaniel had watched, from behind a guarded smile, the commissioner gesturing at beauty as though it were a charnel house.

'This art cannot be considered good,' the man had said, 'when the means of its procurement were iniquitous.' Jeake seemed to walk among effluvia; there was a constant crease in his bloodless nose. 'Look at these bawds and panders.'

Half listening, Nathaniel had marvelled to see so much art: hundreds of works forfeited by the tyrant along with his head. There were portraits by van Dyck, majestic acres of Rubens, including an allegorical Peace with leopards and cherubs and spurting breast milk, autumnal masterworks by Titian (bright-eyed Marsyas flayed by Apollo), and haughty, self-approving princes.

'Where did Charles Stuart acquire a taste for these luxuries?' Jeake grimaced sickeningly. 'I will tell you, Mr Deller. In *Spain*. The very arsenal of Popery.'

Trembling like a husband lifting a bridal veil, Nathaniel had uncovered a woman in furs. The lure of those large eyes! The nudity exalted in its concealment!

'Look at these – a gift from a cardinal, nephew to the Pope himself. So many trinkets to advance the cause of Rome . . .'

Nathaniel's story did not take long to finish; nor the sketch, though it was poorly done. He felt a need to improve it and reached into the birches for his watercolour box. As soon as he opened it, Thomas made a sound of admiration. 'It was a parting gift,' said Nathaniel, 'from my tutor.'

'Is that ivory?' Nathaniel nodded. 'It must have value.'

'So it does, for me.'

'What are you going to do now?'

'Some colour.' Nathaniel scrutinised the ink drawing. He chewed his lower lip.

'I am anxious to return,' said Thomas. 'Is it finished yet? May I see?'

The drawing was no good. Its soul was missing. 'I will use this,' said Nathaniel, 'as my guide for a painting. If you will be patient, let me have a day. Tomorrow evening you will exist in colour.'

'I do already.' Thomas got to his knees, stretched his back and kicked out his legs. His good humour had returned. He tried, with mock slyness, to steal a glimpse at the portrait but Nathaniel turned it over. 'Very well, *doctor pictorus*. I shall try to find some patience.'

'They are all over the heath.'

'A shameful pun.'

'Will you see Margaret?'

'I must.' He made a stage, yet earnest, bow. 'Thank you for making me immortal.'

'Thomas . . .'

The young man turned comically on his heel. 'My lord?'

'Can this last?' Nathaniel disliked himself for asking but he continued. 'This commonwealth you serve. Is it equal to its ideals?'

Thomas frowned deeply: why would anyone doubt it?

'Perhaps,' said Nathaniel, 'it is a dream.'

'It would not be, if enough dreamed it with us.' Thomas doffed his straw hat, all merriment, and set off down the slope.

'You have hope, then,' called Nathaniel after him.

'Hope,' came the reply, 'is having something worth fighting for.'

Deprived of his model, Nathaniel watched the parted ferns resettle. For a time he was empty of thoughts. A sharp itch, from a gnat bite on his scalp, brought him back to his senses. He considered the ink portrait; then replaced it on his sketching book with the unfinished landscape.

Was it a lie already, if two of the five oaks had fallen? In the world they were dismembered; but on paper they survived. Or was that a poet's stale conceit? No image *lives*. The more lifelike an effigy, the more dead it seemed. Then every portrait was a kind of tomb which he, the artist, erected. Nathaniel watched the people at work on the heath. They, who knew nothing of art, were digging for life. *His* business was the dead. Yet the past – the wholeness of those trees at dawn, their shimmering in moonlight – had been real enough once. If God sees all in a perpetual moment, if His creation exists for Him outside Time, then those oaks have never stood there, nor can they ever be lost . . .

Nathaniel's brain rebelled against paradox. The glimpse of divine motion frightened and disturbed him. It was like staring at oneself too long in the mirror, until body and soul begin to diverge and one has to look away, or grip one's face, to keep the two from parting. Let sages and mystics peer into mystery. He was a craftsman, nothing more, in humble service to beauty.

He resumed work.

The cloud had evaporated since he began the

painting. Time and flux were enemies of art. No sooner had one sketched a scene than its shadows moved and the day's complexion altered. Nathaniel, determined to persevere, mixed a salad green for the June oaks. In disgust he rinsed his brush and the ivory plate and made a start on the bruise-coloured heather. He stroked and dabbed without finding his rhythm. The creative trance eluded him. Instead, he felt drowsiness behind his eyes. His head nodded under the pressure.

A bumblebee hummed in his ear. There was drool in the corner of his mouth and his neck ached. He patted himself on the cheek to stay awake and, with his brush, revived a dry swirl of paint on the tray. It was no use. The world of voices and cries, of whispering birches and twittering larks, faded and folded away. The paintbrush fell from his fingers. He snored.

His dream was one of those hateful ones when he went on painting, the brush as large as a carrot in his hand, the paper impossibly coarse and impervious. What his subject was he could not tell: a forest of spirals and scrolls that blackened the page until barely a patch of white remained, like stars in the night sky. Dimly he heard thudding and metal noises, the clanking of diabolical machinery, and faint cries, like a crowd of votaries groaning into pillows.

He woke to the plosion of muskets. At once he

knew where he was and what was happening. His body, clever like an animal, leapt to the ground. He crawled to the edge of the hill.

The rumours, then, had not been idle. Nathaniel watched in dismay as cavalrymen, with clenching knees and thrusting hips, urged their horses through tall heather. More numerous, and spread across the common, infantrymen were rounding up women and children and pushing with their muskets any man who tried to remonstrate with them. There were cries, certainly, from Diggers and shouts of warning from the soldiers; but there was no great violence. Most of the commoners submitted to their fate, wading across country to that barren patch of ground at the river's edge, men, women and children alike carrying their burdens. Between the empty huts there lumbered horse-drawn carts, into which soldiers tossed billhooks and scythes. Nathaniel was too far away to hear the protests of Toby Corbet, who was engaged in a vain tug-of-war with a fat sergeant for his woodsman's axe.

So the gentry had succeeded. Finding the colony against their interests, they had turned the army against it. Those martial hearts must have been cold beneath their tarnished chest plates, for these were not equal foes. A little girl, parted from her parents, wailed at the horses. Old Margery, who was seventy and still strong, had fallen to the sand and lay there cowering from the soldiers' boots.

Nathaniel raged impotently in the dust. He needed urgently to relieve himself.

The important thing was not to panic. He had to think clearly. There were pictures and instruments of value to be rescued from his hut. Nathaniel hoped that his accent and manner might protect him with an officer; but in the disorder an aggrieved Digger, believing his suspicions to be confirmed, might spend his fury on him. Nathaniel's eyes roved swiftly about the heath. It was swarming with soldiers – a body of men vastly out of proportion to the number of commoners. He could not see Thomas anywhere, nor the young parents of the feverish child. Oh, she would perish if they were disbanded! Kicked and beaten into the wilderness!

He decided to come down, to present himself, as an English gentleman, to the nearest officer and then, with licence, calmly collect his belongings. Perhaps, if he displayed his education, he might be spared exposure to the Diggers?

He scrabbled about, rescuing his watercolour box, abandoning his book and choosing, on reflection, to take the unfinished landscape and Thomas's portrait. He would stay low, crouching as he descended, lest a suspicious infantryman should glimpse a head behind the gorse and take a shot. Nathaniel knew what dangers lay in a soldier's apprehension.

Rising on one knee, he scanned the heath for a benevolent officer.

He found Thomas.

What were those brands in his grasp? Nathaniel recognised the pamphlets. The apothecary was waving them, like documents of legal authority, at a pair of musketeers. Nathaniel could not hear what his young friend was saying; but he imagined the frantic appeal to brotherhood, the invocation of freedom, which would sound in those ironclad heads like sedition. One of the soldiers seized the pamphlets and trampled on them. Nathaniel saw, and ached to see, the look of bewilderment on Thomas's face as his rhetoric crashed against cold metal. Then his attention turned to a rearing horse and its falling rider. Three men, Diggers whom Nathaniel did not recognise, had risen from cover, shaking sticks. Immediately, with vengeful howls, they began to beat the fallen soldier.

It was what he feared most. Provoked by the attack, soldiers across the heath began to draw their swords. Several ran to their colleague's defence. Thomas, meanwhile, whose back was turned to the commotion, continued to detain his two musketeers. Interpreting his pleading as a wilful diversion, they pushed him violently. Thomas bounced back, his arms raised in imprecation, and Nathaniel cried out as, without a sound, the musket-butt knocked his friend to the ground.

He ran at once into the thicket. Branches and gorse needles scratched his face. From the path he could hear soldiers running up the hill, and he fought to break through the brittle vegetation. Several yards short of the plain, he stopped to catch his breath and tasted acrid smoke.

They were burning the huts.

He abandoned hope of rescuing his belongings. The drawings made from life, the unsent letters to his brother describing the common – all the evidence of this experiment in living would be lost.

He emerged on the shaded side of the hill. The fighting, which had broken out on the other side, was drawing soldiers to it. Nathaniel began to run, north, away from the disaster. He knew he was afraid. Four words revolved inside his head – *timor mortis conturbat me* – and he began to run through tangled heather, concentrating on this incantation. Twice he fell, snagging his feet on tendons of ling. The second time he lay still, concealed like a game bird, and listened to the cries of women and horses. In his mind he watched Thomas fall again beneath the soldier's musket. It was no use. Fury could not blind him to his fear. He began to crawl on aching limbs: a coward, he thought, reduced to the posture of beasts, making for safety.

Fool! Conceited unreflecting fool! How long had he maintained a vacuum in his mind where thoughts

of tomorrow could not enter? He was of no importance, for the moment, in London. Who cared where
he went, especially at a time of public disorder?
Receiving so little in his father's will had been the
impetus for this adventure. High-minded petulance
had clouded his instincts, but now he recognised all
that was at stake. Radical groups had exhausted their
licence. If it became known that he had lived among
Diggers, the consequences for his art and his family
might be serious.

Three horsemen galloped towards him as he
reached the outer ditch. Formerly it must have been
waterlogged, for he landed on cracked mud.

'Nathaniel?'

'My God – Susannah.'

'Are you hurt?'

She was filthy and dishevelled, her eyes rolling and
her body violently trembling. He held her with an
instinctive need for comfort. Was she unharmed?
Where were her parents?

'Taken already.'

'Are they making arrests?'

'I do not know. We are to leave the land at once. We
have no right to it, they say. Where have you been?'

'Listen – Susannah. Listen to me. You must turn
yourself in.'

She gripped him hard, uncomprehending. 'Let me
stay with you.'

'Impossible.'

'Please, Nathaniel, *please*, I'm afraid of what will happen.'

'Nothing will happen if you go peacefully.'

'They burned our home.'

'Your parents will be looking for you. They will be calling your name, Susannah.'

'But I want to go with *you*.'

He resisted her. She smelled of fear, of sweat and dirt. She crushed her face against his chest. He felt nothing for her but repulsion: a desire to throw her away, to claw himself free of her need. He tried to speak calmly, to assume a paternal authority. 'Do as I tell you, girl. You will be safe, I promise.'

'*No.*'

'If you do not go I will shout. You are evading them.'

He pushed her up the slope, indecorously applying his shoulder to her rump. Dirt and sand crumbled into his face but he continued. As she neared the top of the ditch, he felt her body grow rigid, her will vanishing before the injustice of it all. She fell into the heather without protestation. If she had sobbed, or cursed him, it might have been easier to bear.

Nathaniel, without looking at her, climbed the opposite bank. He could hear lamentations from the river as he crawled through the heather. Shame and fear made his cheeks burn. How long it took him to reach the tree line he would never know. It seemed an hour. Aching in every muscle, he straightened up under the beech trees and walked, with his water-colour box and forlorn papers, half a mile or more, until he stumbled on to a familiar track, brushed himself down as best he could, and began the long walk back to civilisation.

Daybreak

William wakes up in a strange bed. His right arm, autonomous, reaches for the window latch and palpates air. His eyes open on closed drapes; he sees the faded bed-hangings, his clothes in a heap on the stool, and corrects his misapprehension. He lies for a time savouring the restedness of his limbs and the pleasure of his own warmth fomented in the bedclothes. Then he sounds his body, assessing the faint persistent ache in his stomach, the discomfort in his left knee from an injury sustained two weeks earlier while operating the mill hopper. Daylight faint as on a winter's morning seems to rouse all his pains and agues – the familiar tenants of his body.

He remembers Deller; his fall; the portrait.

He sits up, making the bed boards shudder. The guest room has a hushed expectancy: it seems to be listening for something. It is not a presence exactly, a ghostly intelligence, that he senses. Rather an accumulation of years, dust motes of memory, the airy traces of forgotten souls. How many people have rested in this chamber, this place that is, through human transience, many places over time?

Tossing back the bedclothes he notices his tumescence. He pads across the cool boards to his clothes and fastens his breeches over it. Bare chested, he fills the washbasin with water from the jug, his finger catching on a scar at its base. He washes his face and chest; and though he feels no arousal, his member is obstinate. He pulls back the drapes but fails to open the window. It has rusted shut. William sits on the stool and gazes at the grey canopy of sky. He thinks of his father starting work at the mill, and of that other patriarch, ponderous and demanding, sleeping near by, who will expect satisfaction.

What should he think of Mr Deller's last paintings? The clotted paint, the coarse impasto and lack of care in depicting materials suggest to William a sad decline. Perhaps failing sight was to blame for the roughness of the portraits and the murky imprecision of their backgrounds?

Oh, but what does *he* know, a foolish flour boy?

William shakes himself. He has been too long in this house: its shuttered air has corrupted him. He decides to explore the grounds (which were forbidden to him in his youth) and puts on the rest of his clothes. Surely Cynthia will still be in bed? With burrowing feet he mauls the uppers of his boots. He fastens his riding-cloak and is ready to face the new day.

Thomas Digby is running to the window. Quick! He must open it, tearing back the heavy drapes, fumbling at the latch until, thank God, it gives and he lurches after the moving pane into the morning air.

He gasps, his fingers gripping the cold lead of the casement. With each lungful he feels his panic subside. Not today, not *today* shall his heart give way, though a spectral hand seems to compress it in his chest. He knits his fingers as if in prayer and rests his forearms on the ledge. How many mornings have passed since he last felt replenished? When did sleep become a thing to be dreaded, a steep lurch into chaos followed by waking in anguish? He lifts his wrists to admire the pressure marks, those impermanent scars, left by the casement, and tells his trembling body: your plans will come to nothing. What was it you hoped from Deller? Money to finance your venture. Mammon in the service of God.

Thomas groans, not caring who might hear him; for there are sounds of activity in the yard. He makes a fist and thumps himself below the diaphragm, then turns from the window, with its view of glistening meadows and dripping elms, and pads heavily to the water jug. He drinks like a rustic from the vessel's lip, and brings it down so heavily on the table that something breaks. He does not inspect the damage (Deller can afford another) but shuffles to the close-stool to relieve himself. His piss is scalding and malodorous. He wonders whether Nathaniel will be up yet. From the position of the sun, which has risen to survey the storm-sopped countryside, he guesses that it is early. Before seven. No time to breakfast.

He hunts down his discarded jacket. Before its master rises, he will have departed from the house.

He contemplates using the domestic stairs that lead to the kitchen; but they belong to the night and its confidences. He would not swan about, unbidden, like some rake in his place of conquest.

In the corridor, night still holds dominion, as rainwater persists in a ditch, and William must grope his way along the wall until his eyes adapt to the dark. Outside Mr Deller's chamber he stops and listens. The ogre sleeps, guarding his treasure. William foresees a liver-spotted hand rising from the bedclothes, imploring his mercy. Perhaps he might creep in to study the portrait again. Perhaps the drink clouded his judgement and, in the clearness of dawn, he will discover a work more salvageable, a task less Herculean in its difficulty. From beyond the grave, Belinda Deller may yet prove his talent to the world.

Shrugging off the notion, William runs his palm along the banister made smooth, he imagines, by Cynthia's touch. Downstairs the maid must have opened windows, for chalky light sits in puddles on the floor and tapestries heave and shudder. William saunters down the empty corridor, winking at daylight. He can hear cloth being rubbed against stone as he enters the great hall. 'Good morning, Lizzie,' he says.

The woman on all fours, sunk in a frowzy skirt, raises her head.

'Oh, forgive me,' William blurts, averting his gaze. 'I did not know you with your head bowed.'

Cynthia discards the cloth and rises. She rolls down her sleeves, a blush of effort, or is it anger, in her cheeks. 'My father woke twice in the night—'

'I heard nothing.'

'Lizzie sat beside him with a flannel. He has a fever.'

'Nothing grave, I hope?'

'She has barely slept. I told her she could stay in bed for a while.'

'You have risen early.'

'So have you.'

They see each other trying to conceal their discomfort. It is Cynthia who smiles first, inviting William to breakfast. So he sits, leaving his hat on the table, while she goes to the kitchen. When will Deller wake? he wonders. How ill *is* he? A callous hope flickers in William's mind. Perhaps he will not have to give his answer . . .

Returning with bread and whey, Cynthia finds him in a reverie. His chin since last night has grown a shadow. 'Can you be spared?' she asks him as she lays out the food.

'Until your father wakes.'

'And then you will give him the answer he expects?'

William opens his mouth but no words follow. Sensing her mistake, Cynthia pushes the bowl of whey towards his plate and knocks the knife off the butter dish. They eat in silence. With the lifting of bread or spoon, each casts daring glances at the other. To their delight and fright, their eyes touch.

'Would you care,' asks Cynthia, 'to join me in a ramble?'

'I was going to suggest it.'

'Well then.'

At the front door, Cynthia curtsies and lifts the latch. William follows her with his head uncovered. A cool breeze greets them, all the way from the coast.

'Are you cold?'

'No, sir. Are you?'

'The day will be a fine one.' He says this without

authority, for the sky is congested. 'Call it miller's intuition.'

For the first time ever, they are walking out of doors. William strolls beside her, enchanted. When she stops to peer at the sky, she tilts her face strangely, and he realises that she is offering it to be kissed. He knows the ritual that is required of him. 'Madam,' he says, and elegantly bows. He kisses the back of *his* hand, then boldly with licence kisses her lips. It is the briefest of contacts. There is no time to savour the coolness, the yielding of her mouth. He steps back, emasculating the gesture, and puts on his hat. Cynthia waits for him to adjust the angle; then, smiling, she leads the way.

From youthful hours spent pressed to the windows of the manor house, William recognises the abundance of yew. Some of the trees are immeasurably old. Though sombre and funereal, they seem consoling to him. Life which outlasts life. His grandchildren may stroll among them.

A fish leaps in the stock-pond, which clearly is maintained, though the larger pond is benighted by alders. 'It keeps us fed,' says Cynthia, nodding at the expanding rings of water. 'We also keep rabbits and chickens behind the vegetable garden.' She does not add that the gardener and Lizzie poach freely from these supplies. Nor can she blame them for it.

The rollered lawn gives way to tall grass. Cynthia takes William's arm to steer his attention from the beehives crumbling in the shade. He sees inside the vegetable garden, where, kneeling in dry soil, with his hands clasped about a trembling leek, the gardener broods. Fancy absorbs him utterly, or else a mental oblivion, akin to deep sleep, has stolen his senses. Cynthia sees the gardener's indolence but gathers her skirt and continues up the path.

'I recognise that fellow,' says William. 'He used to give me rue for my father's joints.'

'From our herbal bed?'

'Do I betray him in confessing it?'

Cynthia smiles. 'Kind Jem,' she says. William remembers him now from elsewhere. Of course: the bald labourer in Mr Deller's painting. Jem the pea gobbler. Why kind? he wonders.

Cynthia raises the latch on the gate to the herb garden. William sees it rankly overgrown: weeds high as his knee, tides of nettle and burdock half stifling the neglected beds. 'Some parts have been abandoned to wilderness,' says Cynthia. 'There is too much here for one man to master.'

She leads him to the only bed still in good condition.

'Here is camomile. Here sweet woodruff and myrtle. It is not enough for the land to feed us. My father must encounter the world through other senses. So with these,' she says, tickling a parched flower, 'I keep the house stocked with sweetness.'

William can say nothing. From where he stands above her he can see the pale seam of her parting. There is a faint, blonde down above her lip.

'Perhaps your mother knows these,' says Cynthia, crouching in the bell of her skirt. 'Rue – for your father and mine. Wall germander, for the gout. Are you not well, Mr Stroud?'

William clears his throat and stares at an anonymous flower. 'Quite well.' He is a blinking fool. 'Your father is fortunate to have you.'

Cynthia rises. 'Come with me,' she says, 'I have something else to show you.'

❧

Looking into the hall for a crust to eat, Digby surprises a footman picking his nose in the master's chair. He swipes impatiently at the servant's apologies and, seeing that the table is bare, abandons his pursuit. Deller and his wife are nowhere to be seen; but there are sweeping sounds near by and voices in the kitchen. Soon the household in its entirety will rise and he will be confronted.

Retracing his route from the evening before, when wet clothes clung to him like clay, Digby finds the entrance and two maids, neither one Lizzie, on their knees scrubbing the floor with soaking lye. Are those *his* muddy prints? Already abject in their posture, the maids can only nod and flutter their eyelids at him. 'Will you,' he says, 'inform Mr Deller that I . . . that Thomas Digby had to return in haste to the city.'

'Yes, sir.'

'Thank him for his kindness.'

Crouched like cats, their necks taut to watch him, the maids smile. The one on the left is pretty.

'You will see to it that he gets this message?'

'Yes, sir.'

Long lashes. Obedient faces. Digby sees their breasts trembling as they shuffle to let him pass. He struggles with the latch. Their eyes are still on him. The latch yields, the door opens and he escapes into the light.

The sun has gained strength. Already along the cobbled track a mist is rising. He hears splashing sounds and, briefly curious, walks a little way into the garden. It is orderly and well mannered, its shrubs and trees like elegant furniture, and resonant with the clipping of shears and the sough of rakes in soil. So much industry, thinks Digby, to prettify dross. An incandescent bird flames above the pond but he does not look among the trees that extinguish it. He does not see, in the wet grass, the silver filigree left by nocturnal snails, or the blackbird shaking itself in a puddle, beads of water tumbling from its wings.

'Clot. Mooncalf. You will fall in and I will not save you.'

Digby recognises the boy from last night's storm stretched out on his front beside the stew-pond, his face empurpled as he tries to salvage a fishing net from the clutch of water weeds.

'Clumsy ass. You will break it. Try harder.'

An older lad, with a croaking voice and disfiguring acne, stands above the boy, berating him for his trouble and offering no assistance.

Digby declines to intervene. Walking with his head bowed, not to be recognised by the boy, he returns to the courtyard. White doves scatter and wheel about the house as he trudges over mud and sodden straw.

The stables are empty save for his horse. The animal ignores him. Digby searches for the saddle and finds it on a hook, the leather still sticky from last night's rain. He begins to fasten it to the horse's back.

'You would not, then, say goodbye?'

Digby takes time with the buckle before he looks up. Nathaniel Deller is wigless, bare legged in riding boots and wrapped in a brown fur robe. Every affectation is missing, or not yet assumed. From his crumpled face as much as his attire, Digby surmises that he has just risen.

'I had anticipated breakfast with you, Thomas.'

'You should have stayed in bed . . . I hoped you would.' This performance, this mummery of meekness, will not weaken Digby. His horse saddled, he sees to the bridle.

'Must we part unreconciled?'

'I am uncouth,' says Digby, 'at farewells.' It is a base and ill-smelling venue for such a scene. Digby hastens to fasten the straps, his horse placidly nodding; then he props open the partition and leads the animal to the stable door.

Nathaniel steps aside to let them pass. 'My wife was looking forward to making your acquaintance.'

'Please give her my apologies. I really cannot tarry.'

'How far advanced are your preparations?'

The damned fellow clings like a burr. Digby mounts his horse. 'I have three comrades willing to sail with me. You knew two of them. Toby Corbet and Robert Clare. You would think them base fellows.'

'I never thought so.'

'You will, for they turned renegados after Cobham and have tasted the liberty of Salee.' Digby watches, with ignoble relish, the effect of these words on his genteel host. 'In that pirates' republic an Englishman is free.'

'How many throats did they cut?' Nathaniel winces, seemingly at his own words, and pats the horse's cheek. 'Forgive me. I do not mean for us to part on last night's terms.'

'Other men are eager to join us. From the broken

forests, the drained fens. Men driven off the land. We are many, you shall see.'

'And what is it you chiefly aim at?'

Digby looks at him sourly. 'You quote the Soldier's Catechism. You should know.'

'I fear I have forgotten.'

'Do not expect me to say it, for you will only smile.'

'What kind of man do you take me for? I would know your goal, in good faith, that I may offer you my best wishes.'

'Very well.' Digby leans on his horse and takes in, with a sweeping gesture, the lofty ash trees and the sodden house, the dovecote and the swollen brook overhung with sorrel. 'This is so much or little trash awaiting its destruction. The broils of powerful men, none of which improves our condition, are but straw when King Jesus approaches. You *know* He is close. The common was our first attempt to ready the world for His glory. It failed because the Enemy is strong. But not strong enough. So a new place must be cleared and we will find it in America.'

The portraitist takes a step back, into a puddle, and looks down at his mottled robe to shake it dry. It is not a chastened Nathaniel who looks up to meet Digby's gaze but an ageing, sorrowful man. 'I wish you well in your enterprise. Pray for me, that am too much in the world.'

Disconcerted, Digby plucks at his glove. 'So I will,' he says.

'But with joy, as befits your mission.'

'There might be a time for joy . . .'

'Let it be now. Thomas, there used to be a lightness about you. You laughed and caused laughter in others.'

'How do I seem to you now?'

'Heavy as clay.'

Thomas Digby, his hand ungloved, picks at the dead skin on his nether lip. He regards without concern the blood on his finger. 'That was my youth . . .'

'I saw you fall. The day the soldiers came. I saw you beaten to the ground. Forgive me that I did nothing.'

'What could you have done?' Digby pats the neck of his horse. Without willing it, the vision of Belinda Deller enters his mind, lustrous in candlelight, her pale hand posed on the stair rail. She smiles at him in the shadows. He sees her belly swollen beneath her gown.

'Thomas . . .' Nathaniel takes hold of the bridle. How easy it would be to ride him down. 'This thing between us is acquired, not innate. We are not born into enmity. And what men are we if, each pursuing his goal, we fall to hating one another?'

'I do not hate you.'

'Then at least join me for some food.'

'I am used to riding on an empty stomach. I have other fires in my belly to fuel me.'

'You must not stoke them. For the sake of your happiness, do not feed yourself to anger.'

'My happiness is of no importance in this world. We are not born to be happy.' In silence they look to the horizon, at the Kentish mountains of dark, retreating clouds. Digby's horse is restless. Does it sense the journey home, to the fetors of Lambeth? He would be gone: waiting is a great discomfort. But Nathaniel will not relinquish the bridle.

'Shall I walk you to the road?'

'No. Please – don't do that.' From his vantage, Digby sees Nathaniel's baldness: a stark and innocent patch of skin, like a monk's tonsure. It will grow, Digby thinks. Age will steal over us like moss. Like moss, death will cover everything. 'What do you hope for, Nathaniel?'

'Hope?'

'From the new dispensation.'

'To love. To work.' Nathaniel fixes him in the blue ambit of his eyes. 'And you, what will you do now?'

'I shall ride my horse out of these grounds. I shall turn into that woodland there. And disappear from your frame of vision.'

'Into what?'

'Some place far from artifice.'

Thomas Digby clucks and kicks his horse's flanks – forcing Nathaniel to let go of the bridle. Clods of mud, shards of clay, leap from the ground. Both men taste the power of the horse, Nathaniel in his knees, Digby in his bowels. He exults to feel such power at his command, and hears the change in register from cobbles to wet turf as each hoof-beat compacts the grave of his past. He knows the story of Lot's wife and does not look back as he reaches the hawthorns. Faintly he hears Nathaniel calling. 'Be happy, friend.' And fainter, a little fainter, as ancient trees and unchanging hills divide them – 'Remember me!'

From the herb garden they take a gravelled path, down an alley of lime trees formerly pleached and now unkempt. William looks askance and senses that he must be quiet, for Cynthia seems resolute, formidable even. Her hand, which minutes earlier touched his arm, is pressed against her stomacher. She seems to pay him no attention. William unfastens his riding cloak and folds it over his arm. Either the day, or he, is getting warm.

At the end of the alley, where the gravel stops, they find a carpet-walk scythed through a meadow. William looks, perplexed, at the freshly cut stems raked to the margins. He does not know that the walk was created this morning by Jem the gardener, and at

Cynthia's request. It leads, on a graceful curve, to an old, thick, black-trunked oak tree – under whose canopy, in the flattened grass, Cynthia sits down.

She studies William closely. He is sweating. 'This is in the portrait, is it not, Mr Stroud?'

From this angle, with the roofs of the manor house and the stables behind it, the scene is unmistakable. On the ground beneath this tree, the painter placed his vanished wife.

'How do you know?' asks William. 'You told me that you had not seen the painting.'

'Then I am not mistaken?'

'I must have described it to you.'

'There was no need.' Cynthia leans forward, across her knees, and strokes the grass before her feet. 'You see, my mother's heart is buried among the roots.'

William's mouth is parched. He finds himself scanning the ground (in vain) for eyebright.

'She liked to sit here,' continues Cynthia, 'under the leaves. Reading or sewing. Or in simple contemplation.'

William frowns. 'Your father told you this?'

'He did not.'

'Then . . . how do you know?'

'Jem told me. He was just a boy when my mother lived but she was kind to him and he remembers her for it. When she died he was kept at home but Jem's father assisted . . . *We* are not supposed to know.'

William contemplates the innocent grass. What would remain of Mrs Deller's heart, melted into the tree's roots?

'Please,' says Cynthia, 'will you not sit beside me?'

Like a sleepwalker William approaches and lowers himself. The ground is dewless, mossy, and littered with twigs.

'He is dying, you know that.'

'I know,' says William.

From here they can see the neighbouring valley, with its fleece of trees, and the chalk grassland beyond that seems to glow with inner light. The dawn cloud has begun to disperse, promising sunshine. It is the first day of June.

'He wants me to finish the portrait of your mother.'

Cynthia seems not to hear. 'Tell me about your work at the mill. Is it very demanding?'

Disconcerted by her change of subject, William nonetheless obliges. 'Some days it seems as if my father wants me to work it myself.'

'Could you not?'

'Instead of the wind?'

'Oh . . . He expects much of you.'

'I watched them put up the mill when I was a child. Three hundred men it took to build. The kingpost came all the way from the Weald. Is it any wonder that he wants me to continue after his death?'

'But then your art . . .'

'Preposterous that I still think of it. I barely find the time to paint.' William sees clearly how wealth and security, the luxury of time, are pre-conditions for art. How much talent must wither, unseen and fruitless, in all the foundries and cornfields of the world?

'Would you be able,' asks Cynthia, 'to pursue that other vocation?'

'Oh, I have no illusions. Perhaps I could work on the restoration of old paintings – even be a copyist. But what should I do without a friend in the world? Struggle alone in London, a limner, to be indicted for recusancy? Here at least I am a miller. It is a useful trade. Elsewhere I am nothing.' Looking up from his tensed hands, William sees Cynthia distracted, her jaw clenched with emotion. 'Forgive me,' he says.

'For what?'

'Talking of myself.'

He is a man: it is to be expected. 'The child,' she says, 'that she carries in the painting is me.'

'Doubtless.'

'Then I am the death's head in the portrait.'

'Do not say so.'

'It is the truth. My birth was the death of her.'

'Things dying and things newborn.'

'That is too easily said.' She relents and softens. 'Was she happy? In the portrait. Do I look at all like her?'

'I am sorry, I could not tell. Her face is blank.'

Moved, he plucks her right hand from her lap and presses it to his lips. It is cool and passive; he turns it over and kisses the moist palm.

'Can it be done, William? Can you paint it?'

'You are beautiful.'

She snatches her hand away. 'Your *answer*. Can you paint it?'

'Yes. I believe I can.'

William sees, as if a physical weight has been lifted, the relief in Cynthia's body. She takes deeply, into her back and belly, the morning air. He dares to take her hand, more gently this time, and she yields it willingly.

'You will tell him so,' she says, 'when he awakes.'

'It will not be easy. And it will take time, for I have other duties.' William is no longer afraid of his task. It is a dying man's folly, impossible to achieve, and most deserving of indulgence. 'But when the portrait is done, I will abandon my ambitions.'

She bows her head and, with her free fingers, caresses the back of William's hand. What is this called in painting? The hands interlaced: *dextrarum iunctio*.

'Help me, Cynthia. Help me abjure my hopes. Without a true calling, is it not better to renounce the brief delight, the long sorrow?'

'You do not speak of love, William.'

'Would you have a man who is no artist?'

'I would have *you*.'

'And be a miller's wife?'

'Nothing can exist without bread. You are a maker, William. I could be yours and consider myself rich.'

He has yet to unburden himself of all secrets. She spares him the pressure of her gaze and, while she waits, tries to connect each unseen bird with its song. The trilling belongs to a chaffinch, that 'yes-no, yes-no' to a chiffchaff. Over in the vegetable garden, attracted perhaps by Jem's digging, an ouzel cock makes its fluting melody while another, closer by, emits shrill chirps of warning. (It is a fanged and naughty world: she is right to be wary.) Beyond these calls she hears robins and larks, a cuckoo in the wooded valley and, across the illuminated downs, the chanting of a cockerel.

'Cynthia.' William is ready. He consolidates the gesture, sealing her hands in his. 'There shall be no contract between Mr Deller and myself. My services are freely offered, contingent upon nothing.'

'He offered you my hand, did he not?'

'Madam, he did.'

Cynthia lifts her head to watch the canopy moving above them. He wants to kiss the line of her jaw. He does nothing. 'My father must be tired. Let him rest a while, before we go to him.'

Curiously, it begins with his breathing. He hears the struggle of air to pass the congested flues of his throat. A sound akin to snoring, only coarser, like the rattling of chestnuts in a box, ought to alarm him. But there is neither pain nor apprehension. He listens to his life, to the mechanism of his failing body, with curious dispassion. He knows he is not alone in the chamber. He opens his eyes.

'I knew it was you.'

She sits in the waiting chair, in a robe of vestal white. The taint of childbed has been washed from her. She smiles at him, seated unreachably across the chamber, her hands clasped in her lap. From between her fingers peeps an open flower.

'Eyebright,' he says, and he senses the heavy canvas of his face tauten with joy. 'I felt you in my dream. You are beautiful.'

Silently she watches him. For a time he sees his happiness reflected in her face. Then her smile begins to weaken.

'Why do you look at me so? Where have I gone wrong?'

'You know what must be done, Nathaniel.'

'Do I?'

Her voice is as deep and calm as water in a well. 'You must say it.'

'But if he refuses?'

'*Say* it.'

'I must accept William's refusal with grace. And I must not refuse him our daughter.' Is this daylight, this effulgence from her face and robe? Nerves flare in the embers of his body. 'Oh, I cannot.'

'You can.'

'I must not.'

'You must.'

'I have not the faith. With my death your face will be lost to the world.'

'Other faces will take its place, Nathaniel. No man can build a monument against time. To seek to preserve life on canvas is a contradiction.'

How he longs to be released – to have done. But he cannot so long as this obstruction remains in his mind. 'What do I leave behind? I have sold so much and achieved so little. So many retreats and what victories won? What shall future generations say of me, of us – our age?'

'They shall say: these were our forebears. Without each generation we would not be. By each link through the ages we are joined at last with God.'

She sits, young and sainted, his own youth in spirit, contemplating his grief. He will lose her again. The day's night will return, shrouding him in sorrow. 'My eyes,' he says. 'My wife, my eyes cannot water.'

'Be at peace, Nathaniel. Close your eyes and rest.'

With these words all reluctance leaves him. He

believes he nods. His eyelids fall; they flicker instantly, and in that last moment of vision she remains in the chair, her fingers closing about the open flower.

He awakes.

And the world is awash with the singing of birds.